Baroque – 'n' – Roll

and other essays

Baroque – 'n' – Roll

and other essays

BY

BRIGID BROPHY

HAMISH HAMILTON · LONDON

First published in Great Britain 1987
by Hamish Hamilton Ltd
27 Wrights Lane London W8 5TZ

Copyright page © 1987 by Brigid Brophy

British Library Cataloguing in Publication Data

Brophy, brigid
Baroque 'n' roll.
I.   Title
082   PR6052.   R583.

ISBN 0-241-12037-3

Printed in Great Britain by
Butler and Tanner Ltd, Frome, Somerset

To
Shena Mackay

In the note I have added to the beginning of each piece, recording its date of composition and its place of first publication, the *London Review of Books* is abbreviated to LRB and the *Times Literary Supplement* to TLS.

BB

Contents

Fragment of Autobiography

A Case-Historical Fragment
of Autobiography

(1986; Contemporary Authors Autobiography Series, Gale Research Company, Detroit, U.S.A.)

On the last day of 1979 I was ambushed by my closest ally. I experienced catastrophic grief.

The psychological and many of the social constructs through which I had been negotiating my environment trembled. Chunks of my history threatened to tumble into the limbo of non-valid concepts. Doubt and malfunction attended all that was disclosed to have rested, for longer than a decade, on my mere gullibility towards lies and masquerades systematically thrust on me.

In the impact of shock, my personality, always mildly lacking in the narcissism that a psyche needs if it is to hold together, looked likely to fly apart.

I was saved by the love, wits and wit of Michael Levey, my husband, who was himself not unscathed by an act that he, too, had conceived to be inconceivable and that forced us to re-draft in haste both the design and the hour-to-hour logistics of our life; and by another fellow-writer, who, despite the turmoils that beset her at the time, extended me unconditional love and wit.

I sought psycho-therapeutic advice. Friends, including Michael's and my daughter, Kate Levey, took my wreckage in tow and tugged me towards a regained conviction that my work and existence might be, in no matter how nugatory a sense, worthy of pursuit.

At night I still grieved and puzzled. My night thoughts shaped a curious metaphor, by which I was curiously obsessed: without committing any crime the laws would recognise, my assailant had yet contrived to maim and incapacitate me permanently.

By November 1982 I was tolerably sure of not inflicting tedium on them if I accepted invitations from my friends for meetings less snatched than encounters at committees.

Towards the end of the month I spent a morning tending by telephone some of the concerns of the authors' collecting society of which I am one of the founders, dashed through some minimal shopping and went in the afternoon to a committee of writers' trade unions. That evening I left Michael, who is a gifted cook, to his own vegetarian supper and the completion of an article he was writing. In the dark I set out again from our flat in SW5, found a cab and had myself taken to NW1, there to visit Elizabeth Jane Howard in her newly acquired house.

Pleasingly decorated and dressed by Jane, it is a smallish unit of the admirable 1790-to-1840ish architecture of that part of London.

When I had thoroughly seen and taken pleasure in the house, Jane and I walked round to the main road, where she had chosen an Italian restaurant for our dinner, because that would not impose it on Jane but would without fuss cater for my veganism.

It was already lateish, by the standards I observed, on a sharply but handsomely cold night. In minor anxiety I silently bade myself make no delay after dinner about seeking a cab for my return. Michael could not keep late hours because he went off early on weekday mornings, and I had never mastered the skill of sliding into our flat and bed without disturbing him.

At dinner Jane and I talked happily: about the Writers' Guild, our trade union, on whose elected council we have both served, and about politics, which a politick rule in its constitution prevents the Guild from having but which Jane and I both have — on opposite sides, as if to demonstrate why a union of writers must eschew party, but amusingly often in agreement.

We paid the bill for dinner, I fumbling over the numerical and social arithmetic of the tip, and initiated our departure.

There a barrier bisects my memory.

In the next scene to enter my awareness, Jane was absent and Michael present. I questioned him and he replied that Jane was well and had done better than well but he had urged her home because it was beyond two in the morning.

While we held that conversation I was lying on a trolley in the casualty department of University College Hospital.

It was evident that something had not unspectacularly falsified my hopes alike of not perturbing Jane and of not disturbing Michael, but I had no idea what.

A doctor arrived and told me that my skull had been X-rayed and shewn to be intact, that he was about to stitch up the gashes, of which I had been until then unaware, in my face and that I could eventually seek the removal of the stitches from my usual doctor.

I was advised to stay overnight in the hospital for fear of concussion. Michael managed, however, to summon a hired car by telephone and to persuade the doctor at the hospital to let him take me home in it.

3

My first action during the next ten days was to thank and apologise to Jane.

For the rest, I had no concussion and made visits to my doctor's surgery, on the last of which I was relieved of the stitches.

By rehearsing in my mind the events of that day I discovered that I had detailed and continuous memory up to the point where Jane and I were on the verge of quitting the restaurant. The transactions at the hospital informed me that I must have been knocked out by some bang to the head. My memory included nothing that could be a preliminary to that. I deduced that the bulk of my blacked-out interval represented time when I was unconscious but that a section of it was the product of retrospective amnesia, which had crept backwards from whatever the event was that had induced it.

Forgivingly, Jane offered, when I telephoned her, to relate to me what she knew of the incident I could not remember.

Jane told me this.

On leaving the restaurant we decided that the most likely place for a cab was the intersection of the main road we were on, which runs downhill, and the other large main road of the area, which crosses it at the bottom of the hill. Staying on the righthand pavement, we set off to walk there.

Expressly to contradict in advance any figments to which I might seek to ascribe what happened a minute or two later, Jane told me that we were definitely sober and that as we walked down the road we talked 'amicably'.

Before we had walked far I suddenly and without explanation detached myself from Jane's company and ran 'very fast' across the road, which was virtually empty of traffic. When I reached the curb at the opposite side I must, Jane considered, have tripped, though she did not see me do so. What she did see was that I fell down and lay unmoving. 'I thought you were dead', she told me, but when she crossed to me she found me no more than unconscious and bloodied. She did her best to succour me. In doing so she saw and picked up from the gutter or the pavement a ring that had slipped off my finger as I fell.

Jane managed to attract the attention of a policeman, which cannot have been easy at that empty time of night. He walkie-talkied for an ambulance while Jane returned to the restaurant we had just left, whence she telephoned Michael.

Jane then argued her way into the ambulance and sat inside it holding my hand. When the ambulance divulged, by arriving there, which hospital it had taken us to, she again telephoned Michael and told him where to come. When he arrived she gave him my ring.

5

In that narrative the items that impresssed me most but least surprised me were those that incarnated Jane's efficiency and the imaginative quality of her kindness.

A little of what she found inexplicable I could reconstruct, conjecturally, by extrapolation from knowledge and from what I did remember of the evening, particularly my anxiety to reach home before Michael should be asleep.

Many years before, I had lived in that neighbourhood. My sense of direction is deeply deficient. Even so, I must have given informed assent to the idea that the likeliest place for a cab was the main intersection. Equally, however, I will have known that as we walked towards it we were walking away from another intersection, from which, though less probably, a cab might approach.

I think that, on a night virtually empty of traffic noise, my ear, which has the acuteness acquired by a non-driver much dependent on cabs, heard the distinct diesel sound of the motor of a London taxicab somewhere in the distance behind us. There was no guarantee that it would come in our direction or be free if it did, but I conceive that I crossed the road in order to be well placed to hail it on the side of the road it must, if it came at all, drive down. I left Jane abruptly, I think, in a resolution to secure the cab first, should it present itself, and make my explanations and farewells afterwards.

That I ran, by Jane's account, very fast was not odd. No champion sprinter went to waste in me, but I could run short distances tolerably fast. Doing so gave me intense and exhilarating pleasure. Few opportunities to run occurred in the life of an urban intellectual and I was often inhibited by fear of disschevelment, but I took what opportunities or pretexts I socially could. Grandmaternity, which vested me earlier in 1982 and gave me a personal delight I had never expected from something that required neither effort nor even volition on my part, seemed no reason to drop the habit.

My taste for running contrasted with my distaste for walking. True, brought up by parents who walked for fun, I walked ten miles of the Lake District in a day when I was three. The exploit was much cited to me later, but by way of reproach. As soon as I emerged from the compliance and passivity of pre-puberty I discovered that I was bored by walking. I never learned Bernard Shaw's technique of thinking while doing it. In adulthood I evaded walking whenever I could. When it was not to be evaded I did it at a pace that disconcerted most companions except Michael, not because I liked walking fast but with the same motive that made me do most chores at top speed, namely, to have it done with as soon as might be.

Whether the cab I think I was planning to hail truly did come down that road that night I do not know. Jane thought not but understandably, given her preoccupations to my benefit, could not be sure. My conjecture had in any case to stop with my resolve to have it if it did. What happened when my run took me to the opposite side of the road I could not even conjecture, and seven months passed before I became able to.

6

Early in June of 1983 Michael and I dined with Francis King.

Francis was already a friend of long standing when, in 1972, he, Michael and I were three-fifths of the posse of five writers who created WAG (Writers Action Group). Braving multifarious wrath, we invited writers of all types to join and campaign for publicly funded annual payments to authors in proportion to the annual number of loans of their books from public libraries. Seven years of tumultuous struggle later, WAG achieved the passage of the Act of Parliament we sought. We had argued justice to a prime minister and many ministers; we had demonstrated to civil servants the electronic and statistical methods that would compute each author's tally of loans. Even after the Act of 1979 WAG had, through me, to negotiate with the civil servants the administrative machinery they were to set up, and only in 1982, when the machinery was poised, could I write the last of WAG's newsletters to its members and signal WAG's autodestruction.

It was thus a tidy decade of my life that was chewed and eaten by my function as co-organiser of WAG. In *A Guide to Public Lending Right*, a book I wrote in response to an enterprising commission, I recount the history of the quest in Britain, where it was initiated by my father. In keeping with the anti-autobiographical temperament I am at this moment trying to defy, my account is compact and tucked at the end of a volume the bulk of which is a multinational conspectus of rationale and technique. In the title of my book I had to accept and use, since I had failed to shift it, the name which the entitlement and the payments bear in English-speaking countries and under which they were legislated into being in Britain. The name is non-self-explanatory and perhaps positively misleading. Canadian PLR, announced in 1986, is to bear the much more sensible name of 'Payment for Public Use'.

For my devotion to the struggle I have happily received thanks, praise, book dedications and two awards from literary bodies, most of them shared with the other organiser of the campaign. Although I was indeed a happy recipient, the truth is that nothing I did could have been done but for the generosity and patience of Michael and that the whole experience was a grand adventure, exhausting, perilous and heart-wringing but almost always instructive and always completely absorbing.

Francis's dinner party was the occasion of Michael's and my first meeting with him after the triumph and the dissolution of WAG. Francis had assembled Isobel English, Neville Braybrooke and Kay Dick, all of them writers and warriors in WAG's cause, and Penelope Hoare, whose history as a publisher had several times intertwined with mine as a writer and whom Michael and I had last met at a celebration in connexion with a book whose text is by me.

All his guests were old acquaintances of Francis, of Michael and me and, for the most part, of one another. The evening was memorably delightful by reason of those reunions and also through the flexible hospitality as well as the flexible conversation of Francis, who possesses a gift I take to be rare in writers: in talk with him you encounter the tones and themes you enjoy in his novels. He talks about people and does not shroud his acute insights but there is never a suspicion of malice because he is so intently interested in the people concerned. I sometimes think that Francis feels towards his whole human acquaintance and many of the dogs and cats who engage his affection the unresting and unflinching concern that a novelist feels towards his characters.

7

My enjoyment of Francis's dinner party veiled for a time a minor episode I experienced on Michael's and my way there.

Our taxi from our part of Kensington to his took us along

one of the quiet and domestically attractive roads north of the High Street until its route was crossed by the road that contains Francis's house. At the crossroads our driver paused, pushed back the communication panel and asked us if he should turn left or right. I had visited Francis more recently than Michael had and felt convinced that his house was a couple of doors down to the left. From experience in many cities Michael knows that such a conviction on my part argues a high probability that the truth lies up to the right — but not the infallible certainty that would transform my frailty into a useful gift. As it turned out, I was on that occasion correct. Michael made, however, the rational decision and told our driver that we would dismount at the key crossroads he had brought us to and walk the rest. We got out. While Michael stood paying the driver, I strolled the couple of intervening paces to the pavement, where I intended to wait for Michael. When I reached the curb I found it impossible to raise my foot in order to step up.

I waited, deliberately relaxing my muscles, and then stepped onto the pavement without trouble.

I was, however, curiously shaken by an inability of a kind I had never encountered before. On the inner side of the pavement, conveniently just in front of me and conveniently low, there was the wall of someone's front garden. I sat on it for a minute. When Michael had paid the cab-driver, who drove away, he joined me. I told him briefly what had happened and he waited sympathetically until I was enough myself to indicate that we should go on to Francis's.

The pleasure of the dinner party, plus work to be done, hid the significance of the episode from both of us for some days. Then I recognised that I had felt shaken because I had, in fact, experienced something of the kind before, although I could not remember doing so. On the evening I happily spent with Elizabeth Jane Howard I ran full tilt across the main road. I naturally could not stop dead. If, when I reached the curb opposite, I found myself unable to raise my foot and step onto the pavement to wind down my run there, then it was inevitable that I should lose balance and, rather in the manner of a stalled aircraft, tumble headlong.

Within a few days the episode on our way to Francis's proved to be no — as I thought of it — hapax legomenon. Beautiful and useful items from my classical training have fled from my memory, but that scholarly tag in ancient Greek, whose meaning is 'one-off', adheres to the idiom of my thoughts. I expect it is a memorial to my deep unsatisfactoriness as a scholar both of Greek and of my college at Oxford. The college gave me and I was glad to have because it virtually relieved my parents of fee-paying an unusual scholarship that was awarded, at no regular frequency, to an 'exceptional' candidate, who might be reading any subject whatever, whenever one cropped up in the entrance examination. From the moment I set green foot in Oxford I was technically the senior scholar of my college. I did not take the status seriously, considering it only a kindly excuse for giving me money. A natural egalitarian, I thought it would be impolite to go round slapping the tails of my scholar's gown in the faces of colleagues more experienced than I was, and I declined or ignored most of the privileges extended me. Only by disaster did I learn that my conduct was construed as cavalier disregard of my responsibilities.

A persistent though sporadic difficulty in moving about fell on me that high summer of 1983 while I fulfilled two commissions, both greatly to my liking. In the first half of June I was to lecture to a copyright conference in London. At Oxford I had pursued the 'special subject' of formal (Aristotelian) logic, which has given form though not formality to my thinking and arguing ever since and from which I borrowed some of the code names that medieval scholars devised for types of syllogism to use in my novel *In Transit*. At Oxford logic was considered a mere way-in to philosophy, the end destined for undergraduates who began by reading classics. As I had neither aptitude for philosophy nor any belief in its value to anyone, my hope was to swerve from the orthodox route and progress from Latin and Greek to a congenial subject. I explored my chances of becoming a psychoanalyst, resting my case on Freud's advocacy of lay analysis, but the route was of course blocked by the compact in Britain under which the psychoanalytic movement agreed that its practitioners should be people who had qualified in medicine. I did not persist because even my interest in psychoanalysis was outdone by my vocation for writing. I needed, however, something that would let me take a degree without philosophy, and perhaps my inability to find it made the disaster of my academic career inevitable. Logic would have suited me splendidly but for its being linked to philosophy. The immediate practical good I had of it was the mechanical and relaxed delight of doing its puzzles, which served me as, I imagine, knitting serves some of my friends. Only when, as a chairman of a committee of the Writers' Guild, I decided that someone ought to become knowledgeable about copyright, did I discover a second type of intellectual knitting, and I have enjoyed few of my tasks so much as the vice-chairmanship of the British Copyright Council.

My lecture that summer was on the subject of Public Lending Right; and the nub of what I had to tell a copyright conference was that in Britain there is no connexion whatever between PLR and copyright — for the cardinal reason that British copyright law, unlike West German, does not invariably make the copyright in a work the property in the first place of the creator of the work and, even when it is his, does not make it inalienable from him throughout his lifetime.

The end of June and the beginning of July I spent as I have done every summer of my adult life: watching, nowadays on the television screen, Wimbledon. That I should have done in any case. That year I did it more happily because the residue of the bourgeois work-ethic or of nonconformist conscience that can still smoulder in my socialist and atheist breast was tranquilised. Giles Gordon, my friend, fellow-writer, fellow-member of WAG and literary agent, had, not for the first time, secured me a commission to write about the championships. In pursuit of it, he helped me acquire tickets, so that one day of the championships I spent sitting not before the television but, in Michael's company, above the Centre Court.

Even so, I sat uncomfortably. There had developed a stutter in my gait, sometimes, though not always, when I wanted to step onto a pavement. I could find no correlation with any particular circumstance. I slowed down my habit of doing

10

everything at top speed and walked cautiously. I had a number of tall, slim umbrellas in a number of colours. I took to taking one with me whenever I went out. Though it was a fine day, I took one to the copyright conference and leaned on it while I lectured. I felt more foolish still when I did the shopping in a shower and I persisted in carrying an inviolably furled umbrella.

Much as I enjoyed Wimbledon, I found the journey there by underground and bus perilous to my disturbed sense of bodily balance. Soon I found household chores perilous and left many of them to Michael, who had always done his share of them and more. I was incapacitated for days at a time by a sensation I likened to an experience I have, to my regret, never in literal reality had, floating, among up and down currents of air, in an airship.

My doctor, whom I invoked, plausibly suspected my ability to walk was impaired by arthritis and sent me for X-ray to a local hospital. The X-ray disclosed no more arthritis than was 'to be expected' at my age, which was then 54. Before July was quite out, I kept an out-patients appointment at a big general hospital. I was given a thorough-going physical examination by the head of the unit whose clinic I was attending and afterwards questioned by several of its doctors. I did not expect but should not have been surprised to meet prejudice against my vegan diet, but medical fashion had changed. No disapproval met me. I was asked to prepare a two-days' list to shew in practice what I did eat. I went home and typed one, a task for which I had served a long apprenticeship in complying with frequent requests from strangers for recipes or menus for inclusion in 'celebrity' cookery books. I took my list to later visits to the clinic, but it was never asked for. I did, however, politely resist the doctors' description of my airship-like symptom as 'dizziness', because I had no illusion of spinning. I thought that, if I insisted on an exact description of the symptom, one of the doctors might recognise it from a previous encounter and be set on the trail of what the trouble might be.

The trail the doctors pursued first was a false one. At my next visit I was interrogated, in a manner one might expect were one a subversive in a police state, about my drinking habits. Those were and had been for many years desultory, hedonistic and not abstemious but not addicted either. My replies, which were honest, were noted down with presumably deliberately transparent scepticism. I silently wondered whether the medical profession had been seized with a nostalgia for the eighteenth century and was ascribing my difficulty in walking to gout. Eventually, on one of my visits, which I made at intervals of, variously, a fortnight, a month and three months, a doctor agreed with me that that trail was false. I had by then surrendered what seemed to be litres of blood for analysis. My blood vessels and my very blood retreated from the needle and I always had to explain to the nurse deputed to seek another batch that my reason for averting my gaze from her repeated attempts was squeamishness.

After giving up the false trail, the hospital identified fairly quickly an abnormality in my blood: a deficiency of thyroid function. Early one morning Michael and I went to the hospital and collected a prescription for replacement tablets, of which, the doctor impressed on me, I was to take one a day 'for ever'. From the moment I began to do so, I had no more sensations of being in an airship. The doctors assured me that my ability to walk would be restored as soon as my thyroid level was.

After participating in the organisation of PLR and the campaign for it, I observed with curiosity the organisation of the out-patients clinic I attended. Six patients would be given an appointment for an identical time with the same doctor. He would see perhaps two of them, and then a further six, with appointments for a half-hour later, would arrive. The method was systematic and deliberate. Evidently the patients were meant to perceive as well as endure its operation. I concluded that it was designed to deliver to them the message, which I found particularly infuriating as I waited two empty hours with a deadline to meet, that the time of doctors was so precious that they could not afford to risk a moment's delay were a patient not there when his turn came up. Yet there cannot have been any frivolous or merely hypochondriac patients waiting, since an appointment at the clinic could be secured only if your doctor had referred you to the hospital.

At the hospital I attended, there was a purposely designed

waiting-room for the patients. In style it was like a rather shabby airport lounge. You arrived there and were required to present your appointment card at the desk. When you had gone through those formalities, you were at once moved on from the waiting-room and told to sit on a random row of benches and ruined chairs that was cramped along one side of a corridor, with the doors of the rooms the doctors occupied opening opposite it.

The room designed as a waiting-room was thus kept empty apart from the transients about to be sent to the corridor.

On one occasion, when the doctor with whom I had an appointment kept it after I had waited nearly three hours, I mentioned to him the distresses of such a wait. He replied that it could not be helped.

I could discern only two possible purposes in the system. Either the free health service, funded by obligatory taxes, was set up with such political acumen that it was impossible for those who sought to do so to abolish it and they had found it easier to foist on it a system that uttered to its patients a propagandist inducement to use and pay for, in addition to their taxes, private medicine instead; or the system was intended to burnish the egos of the doctors. A doctor whose door opened to admit the next patient would see facing him something resembling the chorus in *Idomeneo*: the miserable and ravaged people had assembled to beg their king to relieve their afflictions. It disturbed me to conjecture that only by such methods could the doctors maintain the self-confidence doctors undoubtedly need if they are to carry their serious responsibilities of action to preserve life or to pronounce it officially extinct. I had hoped that their medical expertise was prop enough.

9

My perilously halting gait made me go no further alone than to our local shops, and squeamishness beset me in relation to hospitals. I was on all my visits to out-patients, at each of which I was given an appointment for the next, accompanied either by Michael, when he could make time free from his directorship of the National Gallery, or, which happened more often, by Shena Mackay. Her company was freely and affectionately accorded, even though she fulfils many responsibilities, including those to her three daughters, and, since she is a non-driver who lives in the philistia of the home counties, my requests doomed her to the unloveliest of rail journeys, on the Southern Region.

It was, all the same, a philistine use to which I put the finest architect of literary baroque, funny and tragic, and the most Firbankian master of surrealism now extant in the English language.

I cannot excuse myself except by need of, precisely, her gifts. Only a great baroque imagination could make acceptable to me the comic and tragic occasions paraded while we waited. The abrasions the system inflicted on my rationality could be balmed and surmounted only by the gift of a great surrealist.

10

It was about six weeks from my first visit to the out-patients clinic to the hospital's identification of a shortage of thyroid in the blood I had yielded with physiological reluctance. Three months after that, when December 1983 was just into double figures, I made another out-patients visit and was told that the replacement tablets had brought the thyroid level of my blood up to normal.

I reported myself gratefully free of floating sensations ('Oh yes, your dizziness') and asked whether I should presently be able to walk. 'Yes', I was told, 'you'll soon be running about like a spring chicken'.

In the new year of 1984 Michael and I met Iris Murdoch, a friend of ours for three decades, for luncheon in the neighbourhood we share with her when she is in town. The only restaurant that could offer us a table was up a flight of stairs. Iris robustly put her hand beneath my elbow and hoisted me up it. All the same, I believed the hospital's forecast that I should soon be able to follow what I still thought of as my usual way of living. I went with Shena Mackay to an exhibition of pictures. The rules, mindful no doubt of what suffragettes once inflicted at another gallery on the Rokeby *Venus*, forbade me to take my umbrella into the exhibition rooms. I found myself at a loss. I sat on a sofa in sight of a painting I particularly liked and waited while Shena went round alone.

In February the Writers' Guild gave a party, in a suite in a high building in central London that I knew to be accessible by lift, where the minister for the arts, who was then Lord Gowrie, was to present to some writers selected by the two trade unions their first cheques for PLR. Leaning on my umbrella, I managed to advance to receive the first and to say the two public sentences needed.

It was the first-fruits of WAG. A further vindication was to follow. The government had set PLR in motion under a scheme containing many flaws, of sense and practicality, which I had been unable to avert. I published my criticisms. I already knew enough, however, to praise its appointment of John Sumison as Registrar and writers already had occasion to applaud his common sense and friendliness. After operating its flawed scheme for a time the government put itself to the legisative bother it could have avoided in the first place and amended the scheme into conformity with what WAG had advised all along. By 1986 only two of WAG's original requirements were not in operation. One needs only an adaptation of what is done in Sweden; the other will take more radical thought and negotiation to introduce.

11

To friendly enquiries at the Guild party I answered what the hospital had told me, that I was on the way to recovery. My belief in that prognosis was sincere but it could not much longer hide from me that the stutter in my movements was becoming worse.

The doctors and the thyroid level in my blood pronounced me virtually cured. Yet I could not walk either fast or with ease. I therefore asked myself whether my disability might be an hysterical symptom. I could trace a plausible aetiology for such a symptom in my distaste for walking, my relation to my mother, who had wanted me to walk for pleasure, and the fact that my pretend-ally turned assailant had robbed me of my favourite means of avoiding walking.

15

I bent on the problem all the rationality I commanded, together with my not unknowledgeable acquaintance with the likelihoods of my own psyche. I concluded that my failure to walk was not hysterical but somatic.

One tiny nexus that conformed with my conclusion was that hysterical symptoms are inclined to mimic true diseases or somatic conditions, in garbled shape if the patient's apprehension of the model is garbled. I was, for a literate person, exceptionally ignorant of medical facts. I had been almost pathologically healthy all my life. I was also squeamish. I did not read even the medical articles and reports in the papers. I could not have named and I could not remember that I had ever seen an example of any condition that my unconscious might have been, even through a garbling scrambler, mimicking.

12

In March 1984 I went, again in Shena Mackay's company, to the out-patients clinic. I explained to the doctors that I was having increasing difficulty in walking.

They asked whether, in the incipiently spring evenings, I went for a stroll.

I tried to explain that I was incapable of strolling even had I been willing.

'This has been going on a long time. You've lost the habit of walking. You must practise walking.'

When the taxi that took Shena and me from the hospital left us outside the house where Michael and I live, I said to her:

'The doctors say I must practise walking. Will you come with me to do some food shopping at the shops on the other side of the road?'

She did. I leaned on my umbrella and from time to time clung to the railings at the front gardens of houses.

Shena carrying my shopping, we crossed back to my home, which is in a handsome stuccoed building, once, I imagine, a posh town house and now divided into flats. A minor portico leads up five or six steps to the communal front door. Through that you enter a communal hall. Staircases lead from there to the flats on other floors. The front door of Michael's and my flat faces you across the ten or fifteen yards' extent of the communal hall.

By heaving on the railings, I mounted the outside steps. Shena took my key and opened the communal front door. Pressing on my umbrella, I mounted onto the final step of the portico and went into the building. I sank onto my hands and knees. Shena, hung about with my shopping bags, could not raise me. I crawled on all fours through the communal hall, wondering whether the occupant of some other flat would at that moment come down the staircase or, having begun to do so, would retreat thinking 'There's that eccentric Lady Levey crawling across the hall.'

Having helped me through an episode she might have invented for one of her fictions and into my flat, where I managed, by heaving on the furniture, to rise, Shena insisted I telephone my doctor.

When I managed to make contact, my doctor came to see me and I implored her to urge the hospital doctors to stop concentrating exclusively on the thyroid content of my blood and to turn their attention to the actual symptom. She undertook to do what she could.

While she was trying, the Persian cat who shares Michael's and my life and bed fell ill. He loves and is loved beyond description. He was a stray whom someone found in her basement, mistook at first for an owl and eventually brought to our daughter who was then living with us.

Because I could barely move, I had to seek a home visit from our masterly vet, to whose skill and expertise I wished I could confide my own case. After a week Darius was happily mended. We had to ask Shena, whom he knows and loves, to fetch him home.

By the second week of April my doctor had managed to procure me an out-of-regular-order appointment at the outpatients clinic. Michael added his entreaties to our doctor's influence by writing to the head of the unit.

Quite as though my difficulty in walking were a recalcitrance on my part, I was told that I was causing great worry and the next stage would be a wheelchair. I was advised to enter the hospital as an in-patient. I was naturally not anxious to do so, but no other way was suggested for the symptom to receive scrutiny. So I agreed and agreed to wait for a telephone call to tell me when to come.

13

Michael received a letter from the head of the unit in response to his appeal. It said that I had repeatedly been advised to go into the hospital as an in-patient but had always refused.

Until my last, irregular visit, which I had made only thanks to my doctor, no one at the hospital had ever suggested to me that I should or even could become an in-patient.

Patients cannot afford to antagonise their doctors, but neither did I want a myth entered in the records of my case. I wrote as peaceably as I could to the head of the unit, saying that Michael had shewn me his letter and that I had never been advised to become an in-patient.

When I was indeed an in-patient, he treated me affably. He never referred to the letters in our triangular exchange.

The relation between Michael and me is one of perfect confidence but my fiction-writing imagination conceived a story, which I have never written, about a couple who lived on the edge of mistrust and were pushed over it when one of them received a letter telling untruths about the other that was written by a figure in authority whose scientific exactitude in relation to facts was taken for granted.

14

My experience of hospital was of pervasive kindness, including the poignant kindness of patient to patient.

A large public ward runs to a time-table apparently designed to keep all patients short of sleep. Shortage of food may be added. These days a menu sheet is distributed on which you may tick the box that allows you to opt for a vegetarian meal. The system does not work if you were not present the day before to make your future option or were undergoing medical treatment elsewhere when the sheets were distributed in the ward. In any case, carnivores and vegetarians alike found the food disgusting.

18

The deprivations visited on the patient reduce his emotional stamina for his dealings with the most rigorously hierarchical society to be found in Britain since the middle ages. The most cheerful social layer is the next-to-lowest, only just above the patients: the ancillary workers, who reign alone at meal times. Their kindness shewed up a social defect I have known of all my life. Neither with nor in its vegan version without milk do I like tea. The English and Irish tea ceremony — and, I suspect, the Russian — is more stately and more inscrutable than the Japanese. Only the context discloses whether 'Would you like a cup of tea?' signifies 'I am sorry for you', 'I apologise for being rude' or 'Let us be friends'. To decline is to slap the face of a well-intentioned enquirer. To ask for coffee instead, as I did in hospital through an addict's need, is to administer a double slap, forehand and back.

I spent five days in the hospital I had visited as an out-patient, with several trips, by sit-up ambulance with a nurse to escort me, to other hospitals, and was then transferred ('We'll lay on an ambulance') to another large hospital. ('The doctor who was to book the ambulance has gone off for the weekend. Could your husband go to the main road, find a taxi and take you there?')

A thin thread of identity was kept alive in me by the constant visits of the people I most closely love, who braved every private inconvenience to keep faith. On my last day in, Anne Graham Bell, whom Michael and I have held dear since we met her when she was working for a firm that published some of my early books, brought me, as she does every year (though this, she said, was a second, later and bonus crop), a clutch of the stout staves which, in her Hampstead garden, miraculously bear camellia flowers, fleshy, vivid, exotic and delicate.

From the daily ritual of weighing the patients, in a chair-scale for those like me who could not be free-standing, I observed that I was becoming thin, a result I should have earlier have been glad to have so effortlessly.

Indian files of medical students practised their gavel technique one by one on the reflexes of my knees. Swarms at a time of medical students settled about my bed. I was asked to walk about the ward for them, which I did leaning on the umbrella I had taken into hospital, and they were asked to note that my way of walking was 'highly characteristic'. I did not know what of.

I was rushed through a series of tests: of the responses of my nerves, of my vision; electrodes were glued to my scalp; I was dunked in a brain scanner.

I went home for a fortnight and returned to the same ward and the same bed of my first hospital for a lumbar puncture. It was done, by a kind doctor, without pain to me, without provocation to my squeamishness, since it all went on behind my back, and without fear since the doctor acceded to my request and told me in advance each act he proposed to perform. The hospital averted the dire headache other patients have suffered as a result of the procedure by keeping me lying flat for twenty-four hours. Then I was allowed to go home.

15

A better read patient would, I dare say, have guessed what tentative diagnosis the tests were designed to confirm or deny.

I was told that I had multiple sclerosis: or, rather, that the results of all the tests thoroughly conformed with my having it — a presumably legalistic formula that reminded me of my sending down. My college wrote during a vacation to say not that I had been sent down but that I should be if I attempted to return to Oxford when the new term began.

The remnants of my ancient Greek told me that sclerosis was a thickening. I did not realise that the thickening in question was of the very nerves. Neither did I know that the cause of the disease is one of the puzzles of medicine. I asked the doctors what caused it. 'You had a very severe illness in childhood.' 'No, I didn't.' 'You mean you don't remember. You were too young at the time.' 'I mean I specifically and explicitly remember that I was exceptionally healthy as a child and that my parents repeatedly and specifically told me that that was so from the moment I was born.'

16

In the search for the cause of multiple sclerosis and other mysterious diseases, and for a means of curing them, it is vital that no animal, human or non-human, be tortured or killed.

That, which I have given a good chunk of my life to saying in print, I now say with the authority of a person with a personal stake in the matter. It is not my personal stake that makes my anti-vivisectionist argument correct, but unless you can cite it you are open to emotional challenge by the emotionalists who support vivisection.

Human society has consistently asked itself the not-to-the-point question, 'What is the life of this rat or the freedom from terror and agony of that monkey worth to us?' The pertinent question is what they are worth to that monkey or this rat. His life is the only one that is open to him. His awareness, which you can so easily suffuse with torment, it the only one he can experience.

The vivisectionist fallacy is a wilful and anti-scientific denial of the unique singularity of each individual sentient animal. To persist in asking the wrong question is fascism. You convince yourself that the life and happiness of this socialist, homosexual Gypsy-Jew, whatever it may be worth to him as a unique possession, is worth nothing to you.

17

Vivisection would still be a fascist atrocity even did abandonment of it, as its advocates pretend, place on you the responsibility of abandoning the hope of solving puzzles and discovering cures.

In reality, however, the method, in which society has invested not only millions of lives but millions of pounds and man-hours, has produced results far from commensurate with the investment. Adherence to an expensive, luridly impressive and old-fashioned orthodoxy inhibits scientific imagination.

The answer to some cardinal puzzles about multiple sclerosis is likely to emerge from an imaginatively used computer — an instrument that is, in many respects, an automated version of a formal logician.

In Britain I have found only one enquiry into the disease that explicitly forswears the torture of animals and thus makes itself the only organisation to command the allegiance of anti-fascists: the Naomi Bramson Trust, which operates at Newcastle-on-Tyne.

It was there that my anti-fascist daughter was examined and learned that, although it clusters in families, the disease is not directly inherited (a dictum I half-understand thanks to the tuition of statisticians on the subject of PLR) and that, to our relief, she is extremely unlikely to contract it.

To find the cause of that or another puzzle-disease, it is necessary first to compile comprehensive statistics: the number of extant persons in Britain with the disease, properly broken down according to their age when they experienced the first symptom, which may be recognisable as such only by hindsight, their sex and where they live. Only when those facts are gathered can an accurately representative sample be chosen, to whom you can put questions, starting with the most likely and working down, if need be, to the seemingly irrelevant, so that by computer-sifting of the replies you can eventually isolate a factor common to all the cases. It will, of course, be necessary to listen to the replies rather than assume you know better.

As a multiple sclerosis case I refute one medical myth I heard before my case was diagnosed, namely that people are safe from the disease once they have passed forty.

I conceive that it would be possibly useful to ask the subjects in such an enquiry whether they were precocious, late or average developers; whether they have reason to think that they have any specific natural immunities to infectious diseases; and whether they had, as children and as adults, good or mediocre health up till the time they contracted the disease.

I am not sure whether my own experience suggests to me that it would be worth asking 'In the five years before you contracted the disease did you undergo a major emotional shock?' The answers would be difficult to evaluate, since one person's shock is another's frisson. Given the chance, my assailant no doubt would have wished the disease on me; but I find it impossible to believe that it can be induced by malign wishes or witchcraft. The answer to the question of what does induce it may well drop out of the accumulated and sifted replies to a question as seemingly wayward as 'Do you like blackcurrants?'

18

When my night thoughts were obsessed by the metaphor in which my assailant had maimed me, the disease that did in reality maim me had not yet produced a single symptom apprehensible by me, let alone by outside observers. The metaphor gave expression to my realistic recognition that the fury I suddenly encountered was, in psychological content, murderous, though it did not issue in a literal murder. For that perception I might have found a dozen different metaphors. Yet my thoughts returned to and dwelt on that single metaphor every night.

Although there were no symptoms of it, I find it easy — indeed, almost obligatory — to believe that the disease was already attacking me and carrying out its stealthy work in my body. I find it possible, though no more, to believe that the clandestine actions the disease was provoking were accessible to me by sensations that I was not consciously aware of, just as a person may perhaps unknowingly keep track of his digestive processes. I find it hard to believe that my subterranean awareness of clandestine processes was accessible to my unconscious, which framed the metaphor. I think I find it virtually impossible to believe that the metaphor thus framed was one that contained an objectively correct account of the results the disease had not yet made manifest. Before it was diagnosed in me, I heard the disease named once, in connexion with the medical myth about the age at which it attacks; I had probably read the name once or twice in passing; I had no concept of its symptoms. My obsessive metaphor was perhaps occasioned simply by my obsessive and fearful state of mind, but I do not think it entirely unthinkable that intimations from my body were alerting my mind to facts it did not know.

19

If it is random bad luck to be struck down by the disease, it is random comparatively good luck to be struck down in a welfare state.

My umbrellas are returned to the umbrella stand. The

23

DHSS lends me a device that resembles the mythical monsters whose existence Lucretius shewed cogently and mellifluously to be impossible: its upper half is like the handlebars of a scooter and its lower half like the wheels of a tricycle. By leaning on it, I quasi-walk about our flat. At noon on weekdays I go to the next room, climb into the electrically motivated wheelchair, whose batteries Michael recharges for me weekly, and drive to the kitchen where he has left Persian-cat-food ready in the fridge.

The wheelchair, which the technicians who delivered it to me called by the lethal name 'the electric chair', pays me out for having written a novel with the title *Palace Without Chairs*. Only in a palace without furniture of any kind, instead of in our narrow-corridored flat, could its virtuosity be fully used. I was given the loan of it in exchange for an undertaking never to take it out of doors, though I am allowed to seek special permission to take it abroad. How I could do that without taking it out of doors I cannot work out unless the entrance to the Channel Tunnel were to lead through our floorboards.

The occupational therapist has had a discreet handrail placed in our portico. By clasping it with one hand and leaning on one of the tripod sticks I have on loan, I can follow the system the physiotherapist coached me in and descend the stairs. A companion carries down the non-automated wheelchair that is allowed to go out and that folds. Michael or Shena pushes me out for an airing or loads the chair and me into a cab, which, on the strength of my GLC-invented taxicard, will take us at subsidised rates to an exhibition of paintings and which is of all vehicles the easiest for a cripple to climb into. I do not visit operas and concerts; even if there were dispensation for my wheelchair, there could not and should not be any for my need to move about after ten minutes' immobility; but music is, happily, available to me at home.

That I can work — and do, constantly, for understanding editors and publishers who do not nag me for delivery — I owe to friendship. In addition to her novels Gillian Freeman writes scripts, which are often exigent about format. In her exploration of word processors she saw a portable one so small that she divined that I should be just about able to transfer it to and from a mobile worksurface. Since she is one, she knew what a

24

writer would want of such a machine, and she put me in touch with the firm from which I bought it.

My doctor, who sends me prescriptions by post when I ask, has passed on to me word of my being allowed to visit the out-patients clinic should I need to. I have made only one visit, soon after diagnosis. I was told there was no pressure on me to comply but I was asked to spend a day at the hospital standing or sitting by to serve as a specimen for students taking exams. The service was asked of me, but I could not have given it without passing on the burden to Michael or Shena. So I said No.

20

That is the chief curse of the illness. I must ask constant services of the people I love most closely, of whom I require my three meals a day and constant water and eternal coffee, by vacuum flask when I am alone. I cannot do any service to friend or stranger without passing on the burden of doing it to the people I love. They must buy me the card and the stamp before I can reply by polite postcard to a stranger's letter.

Sporadically it is, in its manifestations, a disgusting disease. Also sporadically, it has another anti-social result, wrapping one suddenly in an inexorable fatigue like a magic cloak of invisibility. Its sporadicness destroys the empiricism by which normal people proceed without noticing they are doing so. The fact that yesterday I sat on the edge of the bed and managed to open the drawer that faced me argues nothing predictable, in either direction, about my chances of doing exactly the same action today or of falling to the floor and staying there for a quarter of an hour before I can lever myself up.

In the limbs worst affected, which for me are the legs, it induces a strange, unnatural numbness, which does not preclude pain or even the further numbness of cold but makes one inhabit a surrealist world. As I sit in a chair or lie in bed at night, I cannot tell whether I have crossed one ankle over the other unless I look to see.

It is an illness accompanied by frustration. Writing, even by shorthand, has always been slower than thought. The time-lag is unimaginably magnified by the delays of crippledom. The

25

reference I must check is in a green book on the left of the shelf to the right in the room next door; yet, though I can slowly limp through to its vicinity, I cannot reach it and could not carry it away with me if I could. That makes another service I must ask of someone I love. That ornament is askew. I cannot reach that either. That makes two further services I must ask.

It is an illness that inflicts awareness of loss. The knowledge that I shall never be in Italy again is sometimes a heaviness about me like an unbearable medallion that bends my neck.

Yet the past is, except through memory and imagination, irrecoverable in any case, whether or not your legs are strong enough to sprint after it. All that has happened to me is that I have in part died in advance of the total event.

The obverse of the medallion that weighs me down is my luck in having the opportunity, and my wisdom in taking it, to know so much of Italy. While my going was good I visited the Soviet Union; I have been in Samarkand in a blizzard. I have been in the incomparable city of Lisbon; in Prague; in Reykjavik; in Budapest. When Michael prepared his book on Ottoman art, I went with him and perceived that the form of the mosque is one of the great inventions of architecture, the twin to the baroque.

I am the grand-daughter of an architect, but I never met him and I do not think it is through heredity that architecture moves me. The raw intellectual material of architecture is the relation of one space to another. How have I so great a sense of architecture when I have so little of direction?

I have set foot in places that are, and not only to classical scholars, holy.

The three of us stood on the plateau of wind-racked grass at the top of the site of Troy. To one side were the quasi-terraces cut by the excavation to disclose the layers of the successive cities.

Perhaps because we were three in number, three Turkish — three Trojan — children circled us at a distance. The oldest was a girl of perhaps eight or nine. Walking slowly, with an almost processional dignity, they approached us direct. They were seriously beautiful, without a touch of the urchin, and seriously serious. Unspeaking and unsmiling but with courtesy they gave us three long-stalked vermilion poppies plucked from among the grasses. They were keeping the oldest social rule of Greeks and Trojans alike, that you must give an hospitable welcome to strangers, a rule still in observance in countrified parts of both countries. I thanked them in a couple of sentences of formal English, whose sense I knew they would not understand but whose tenor I hoped they would. We realised that we were involved in another high Homeric custom, an exchange of gifts between notables. We rapidly discussed whether we should give the children money but hesitated because of the seemingly lunatic generosity we had already noted to be a debonair matter of self-respect in Turkey, especially among people who could patently not afford it. The only givable alternative we had with us was a great assembly of boiled sweets, big cellophane-swathed ovals in the deep, not quite transparent colours of jewels which we carried as protection from thirst on the dusty drive through Asia Minor. None of us could be sure that the sweets were the right choice. I gave some clutches of them to the children. They withdrew a little way, presumably to indicate that they were not seeking more from us, and looked at us courteously. After a couple of minutes they walked with slow dignity away.

I am the ancient Greek ghost, sent down in the ultimate sense, who on meeting Charon proffered a boiled sweet as the price of the ferry passage.

Reflexions

Fan-de-Siècle

(LRB, 1983; Murasaki Shikibu: Her Diary and Poetic Memoirs, *a translation and study by Richard Bowring, Princeton University Press;* Evelina, *by Fanny Burney;* The Journals and Letters of Fanny Burney, *Volumes VIII to X, Oxford)*

A small ad in *Private Eye* seeks a companion 'sexy, feminine and discrete'. Siamese twins, I suppose, need not bother to apply. It is harder to divine why this translation of Murasaki's *Diary* renders one passage by the words: 'This is not to say that her women are always so genteel; if they forget themselves they can come out with the most indiscrete verses.' Perhaps, in becoming conversant with Japanese to a degree he makes plain even to me who know not a syllable of the language, Richard Bowring has forfeited some command of English. That looks all the likelier when he skids into bad grammar: '. . . sent to whomever was to copy out the story'. Or perhaps both the 'indiscrete' and the 'whomever' are misprints. If so, there is something moving in the persistence — and the persistent justification — of literary fears. It is roughly a thousand years since the son-in-law of the Emperor of Japan filched a copy of Murasaki's novel from her room at court and she recorded in her *Diary* the quintessential literary dread that it might be an inaccurate copy that 'would hurt my reputation'.

She was a widow in her thirties, already famous as the author of that rumbustious, read-on yet delicate novel *The Tale of Genji,* when she joined the entourage of the Emperor's daughter in the combined capacities of lady-in-waiting and literary lion. Her *Diary* of (chiefly) court life is, Mr Bowring considers, more probably a reconstruction in tranquility than a compilation of day-to-day entries.

31

It opens, in 1008 AD (Kanko 5 in the Japanese calendar of the time), with what might be the beginning of the scenario for an extra act to be interpolated between Acts One and Two of *Madama Butterfly*. It is marred but not ruined by touches of the seedsman's catalogue in the translation: the beauty of the imperial palace in the autumn 'defies description', and the foliage beside the lake becomes 'a blaze of color'. As night descends, chanting begins; then gongs sound; just before dawn, a procession of 20 finely-robed priests carries 'the consecrated objects' across 'the magnificent Chinese Bridges in the garden'. The Emperor's daughter is about to give birth to her first child.

In what Mr Bowring sees as a bit of political good luck that strengthened the dynasty and Murasaki describes as the occasion of general euphoria, the princess is safely delivered of a son, one of whose first acts is to pee on his father. He is truly to the manner born at this court, which resembles that of Edward VII in its mixture of rigid and often unfathomable rules (women waiting on the princess must wear their hair dressed upwards, only people of certain ranks are entitled to wear clothes of the 'forbidden colours') with simple-minded horseplay. During one ceremony, a drunken Provisional Middle Counselor 'started', Murasaki records, 'pulling at Lady Hyobu's robes and singing dreadful songs'. During another, 'the younger women were greatly amused,' she notes, when the ceremonial rice was thrown and a religious dignitary hid his face and his (presumably bald-shaven) head beneath a fan to avoid being hit.

Murasaki is clearly writing for publication and probably with propagandist intent. She does not abstain from the sort of flattery royalty usually exacts from its pet writers: 'I do find it extraordinary how she can . . . make me quite forget my troubles; if only I had sought solace for my unhappiness by taking service with Her Majesty much earlier.' Even so, this is recognisably the world of *Genji*, attractive yet enigmatic in its perhaps over-refined aestheticism, and recognisably, if one dare judge through the hazards of translation, the work of Murasaki. The formality is pierced by the personal ('"Is this the moon that used to praise my beauty?" I say to myself . . . Then, realising that I am making precisely that mistake which must be avoided, I become uneasy and move inside a little, while still, of course, continuing to fret and worry') and by an almost fin-de-siècle or indeed fan-de-siècle dying fall ('the fans women had then were so beautiful'), as well as by the perennially literary experiences: 'I tried rereading the Tale, but it did not seem to be the same as before and I was disappointed.'

It is a world where you expect to be judged by the colour as well as the elegance of the characters you write/paint, and where you are probably writing/painting them in the course of addressing, to lover, friend or mere acquaintance, a five-line poem (discrete or indiscrete, as the editor might say), to which the recipient is expected to supply a rejoinder in kind, perhaps borrowing your brush and improvising it on the spot. Such poems and such pairs of poems by different hands are the core of the second Murasaki document translated in the volume, her *Poetic Memoirs,* her own collection of poems by and to her, with her brief note on the occasion of each, supplemented by Mr Bowring's longer notes on dates, texts and word-plays in the originals. The greatest play, however, is on the pathetic fallacy. Sometimes a poem distils its emotional content from the colour and shape of the single flower that might accompany it as a gift, but for the most part the verses go, in a phrase (I think) of Keats's, gaping after weather, with the result that an exchange of poems is often a more formal but less ritualised version of the exchanges that take place in England a million times a day where each speaker makes a statement about the weather that is at the same time a statement of his own mood.

I went to the Kamo shrine. The dawn was beautiful; all it lacked was the singing of a wood thrush. Catching sight of some interesting trees at Kataoka, I wrote:

> While waiting
> For the bird to sing
> Shall I stand
> In the grove at Kataoka
> And feel the drops of dew?

33

Unlike the imperial new-born, the translations in this volume are swaddled in nearly impermeable layers of editorial matter: prefaces, appendices, groundplans and some murkily reproduced prints for the elucidation of the palace topography, running commentaries. The commentary on the *Diary* is interleaved, page by page, with the translation, which leads to some crowded left-hand pages and some totally blank. The commentary on the *Poetic Memoir* is interspersed with the translation but given in smaller print. The poems themselves appear in double columns: on the right, the translation; on the left, what is presumably a rendering, in the Western alphabet, of the sound of the Japanese original. Apart, however, from the bar printed over some *o*'s, which I take it indicates that they are long *o*'s, there is no clue to the pronunciation, let alone the accentuation, of the sounds. Is *nao*, for example, a word of one syllable or of two? Unless, therefore, you know Japanese, in which case you don't need it, the device seems lavish rather than informative.

Of the information that is given unambiguously, quite a lot seems designed chiefly to assure scholarly colleagues that their contributions have not been overlooked. Conspicuously, the editor lacks the eye of a Japanese poet: he confuses the wood with the trees or, to translate the poetic fallacy, confuses what could be safely stowed in tiny print at the back for the gratification of the scholars concerned with what a modern, Western reader actually needs to be told if he is to feel his way round these exotic literary conventions. I have read *Genji* in two different translations and I incline to think that Murasaki is a great novelist. She is certainly a highly remarkable one. It is a crying and philistine shame that no artist was called in and given the power ruthlessly to turn this publication into a real book.

I was reflecting how different was the response to novelists of the 11th-century Japanese royal house from that of our own dear Hanoverian-and-after monarchy when I was stopped in my unfair tracks by the memory that in fact something very like Murasaki's experience did happen to Fanny Burney. She was swept, as Second Keeper of the Robes, into the train of Queen Charlotte, George III's wife, when she too was in her thirties and famous as the author of two best-sellers, *Cecilia* and her rumbustious, read-on first novel, *Evelina*, which Oxford has now reissued as a World's Classics paperback. The potential for psychological delicacy and intellectual irony of the genre that Fanny Burney virtually invented in *Evelina*, though she neglected to take it out of the corset of the epistolary form, through which her energetic plotting and her exuberant social observation burst most implausibly, was exploited not by herself but by Jane Austen, who accorded the pioneer generous credit in her great flight of ironic rhetoric: 'Oh! it is only a novel . . . It is only Cecilia or Camilla' (both of which are by Fanny Burney) '. . . or, in short, only some work in which the greatest powers of the mind are displayed . . .' Surely the offer of a free quote from Jane Austen must soon entice some publisher to reissue *Cecilia* and *Camilla*?

Fanny Burney was not a great writer, but she was thoroughly a *writer* and an exceptionally vigorous one. If it did not occur to her to break the epistolary mould in *Evelina*, it was probably because she was herself in real life such a good and unpretentious letter-writer, interested in, and therefore interesting on, everything that came to her notice. Oxford has now pursued, with Volumes VIII, IX and X, its admirable enterprise of a complete hardback edition of her letters (together with some letters to her) and the historical and family memoirs she composed out of her superabundant literary energy. The editing is exemplary and, for what you get, the prices are shockingly low, which I hope indicates that the publishers mean to sell to individuals as well as libraries.

An individual who is constrained (or so conditioned to expect books to be cheap as to believe himself constrained) to limit himself to one volume would be wise to pick Volume VIII, where Fanny Burney, married to the royalist Frenchman Alexandre d'Arblay, vividly reports, at first from Paris and then from Brussels, those exciting and perilous Hundred Days of 1815 when Napoleon (or the 'tiny Tiger', as she and, the editors say, contemporary cartoonists often call him) burst out of exile and raised an army. She reports, via Princess Elizabeth, to the British royal family, using, lest letters be intercepted, a code that would have delighted Murasaki since it consists of calling the personages of the royal family by such names as Magnolia and Honey Suckle. She notes that in

France it is perfectly correct for a woman to receive a man caller in her bedroom — a social convention that, when practised in England by a visiting Frenchwoman, makes ripples in the plot of *Evelina*. She laments that the French translation of her latest book, *The Wanderer*, is, 'I am told, . . . really abominable'; Murasaki's fear of misrepresentation by copyists has reduplicated in the modern world. She writes to her son, an undergraduate at Cambridge, who is in immediate danger from an outbreak of fever caused by a bad drain at Jesus College and in constant danger, his parents fear, of turning out a lout or a ne'er-do-well. (He got his own back later by becoming a clergyman.) Above all, she exchanges letters with her husband, who, having joined the army of Louis XVIII, was traipsing about the Belgian countryside wearing a plumed Greco-Roman helmet that made little boys laugh as he passed and who boldly and honourably, though foolhardily, since it looked at the time as though Napoleon was going to win, signed his name to the proclamation by which he sought to induce Napoleon's soldiers to desert to the king.

Though seized with military fervour, d'Arblay spent the war safely at Trèves. It was Fanny who was in Brussels during the Waterloo campaign. Her letters have become a prime historical source for the tension beforehand ('How awful is this pause! How, and in what manner will it terminate?'), the military build-up ('The encreasing quantity of British troops in this Town just now is amazing'), the Duchess of Richmond's ball, which she did not attend but of which she immediately obtained an eye-witness account, and the dreadful straggling back into Brussels of the wounded soldiers after the battle.

She writes to d'Arblay in a fluent macaronic: '. . . & with no time on the instant to endeavour to faire passer une lettre à Mme Deprez'. Even her bits in English sometimes take on a French construction: 'The brave scotch Highlanders are proudly amongst the foremost. They all conduct themselves here in a manner the most exemplary.' *His* excursions into English go barely beyond a 'my dear Fanny' and a rare 'Ma santé est excellente mais, my spirits are not so.' For the most part he writes to her wholly in French.

Fact Sheet

(TLS, 1985; The Button by Daniel Ford, Allen and Unwin)

Prompted by the boast in a fact sheet to the effect that the military expect telephones to be answered 'right now', Daniel Ford asked the brigadier general who was shewing him round to demonstrate one of the telephones at the battle-station desk. Its purpose is to link the battle station to the Pentagon, which, should the battle station report to it a belief that the U.S.A. is under nuclear attack, then uses the same line to assemble a telephone conference between commanders and the president. The general, Mr Ford says, 'picked up the phone briskly and punched the button next to it, which lit up right away'. Nothing else, however, happened. After some seconds of nothing, the general hung up.

The non-incident took place in the command post of NORAD, the correctly named (since it is staffed by the Canadian as well as the U.S. air force) North American Aerospace Defence command. The post is housed in a dynamite-dug cave inside the Cheyenne Mountain, a Rocky mountain in the region of Colorado Springs. After the non-event Mr Ford sought the explanation. NORAD headquarters told him by letter in February 1984 that the telephone in question is capable only of receiving incoming calls. Were that the true explanation, it would make nonsense of the system. The same mountain houses computers that are supposed to analyse early-warning data. On their analysis NORAD depends in assessing whether or not the U.S.A. is being attacked. If NORAD's link with the Pentagon works only in one direction, the defence of North America is counting on intuition to alert the Pentagon when it would be advisable for it to telephone NORAD. It seems a little more likely that the general in question gave the correct explanation when, in April 1984, he rebutted the statement made by his command and counter-claimed 'I just flat screwed up', inasmuch as 'I didn't know that I had to dial "0" to get the operator'.

Daniel Ford, economist and contributor to the *New Yorker*, locates his intellectual point of departure in a publication by an Australian academic. It is, however, the telephone story that aptly begins his narrative of his exploration of the communications network on which the supreme powers of the U.S.A. would be wholly dependent for receiving information and issuing orders in the event of nuclear war. In case the war plan of the Soviet Union includes, as the war plan of the U.S.A. includes, the policy called, with gallows panache, 'decapitation', namely the destruction by aimed missile of the other side's leaders before they can act, provision is made for two aeroplanes to take off bearing respectively a battle staff and the president. The latter the editor of the *New Yorker* might justly gloze 'Who he?' The advance of technology has so diminished the margin by which early warning can truly *be* early that the presidential function is expected to need to be performed by substitutes up to or beyond the limits of the line of succession ordained by the constitution. Both aircraft are equipped to use several distinct methods of communication, one supposedly sure if another fails, for making contact with each other, receiving information from the ground and sending orders to whatever ground-based people or automated weaponry might still exist. However, the method of communication that seems to have the greatest chance of working in the unthinkable circumstances requires each of the aircraft using it to tow a five-mile-long radio antenna behind it. Even in the conditions of peace it often snaps off. Even if it stays attached it makes the aircraft difficult to manoeuvre. It seems unlikely that the two aircraft could fly, let alone communicate, in a nuclear attack. If they managed to fly, they would probably manage neither to be refuelled in flight nor to find an airfield sufficiently intact for them to land.

Mr Ford's is not a discussion of the ethics or the politics of deterrence but an examination of the mechanisms on which it relies. It uses only published or named and checkable sources.

38

That the general who tried to use the NORAD telephone bears the first name Paul in the text but Robert in the source notes is, alas, too flimsy a reason to suppose him fictitious.

By spectacular logic of the kind needed for unravelling a snarl of string Mr Ford traces the chief vulnerability of the U.S.A. to its dependence on a communications system of which some critical tracts are in private ownership and the whole uses apparatus liable to malfunction, to misinterpretation and to disruption by accident and by inexpert use. Vulnerable to such hazards, the system is immensely more vulnerable to deliberate attack.

To this multiple vulnerability, compounded by inter-service rivalry, he traces the development of the present situation, where strategic realism edges the military, and the military edge the politicians, nearer and nearer to a policy of first strike. We are no longer caught up in a simple, though infinitely dangerous, nuclear armaments race. It is turning into a race to determine which side will attack before it is attacked.

Apart from an excursion on hair-triggers in fire-arms, whose value as an analogy he is less successful at explaining than its technical content, the book is succint and elegant. Its few inelegancies are wished on it by the professional jargon of its subject-matter, which in a perhaps symptomatic reversal of concepts says 'survivable' when it means capable not of being survived but of surviving. For the most part Mr Ford translates technical material into literate, wholly comprehensible and in places wry discourse that does not dishonour his epigraph from Robert Musil.

Citizens with the good luck to live in states that accord them votes incur the responsibility of informing themselves of the facts Daniel Ford sets out pellucidly. There are stirrings, which will surely increase swiftly, towards an insistence by electorates on an acceleration of diplomacy. Human civilisation, which is not confined to democratic countries, can survive only if its diplomatists exercise greater skill than its technicians. Humans have been myth-making for thousands of years about an end to the world. Technology has now given them the means to make their myths come true.

39

It is clear from Mr Ford's book that the way the world ends is now on course to be both with a whimper and with a bang — and, indeed, with pop: a telephone that rings (or at least lights up) but who's to answer? The strategy we vitally need is one able to defeat human myths and human nostalgia for the primal slime.

To Be Continued

(LRB, 1980; The Mystery of Edwin Drood, *by Charles Dickens, concluded by Leon Garfield)*

The boldest way to supply the missing half of *Edwin Drood* would be in the idiom of the present time. Such a course would nowadays come naturally or at any rate fashionably to an architect were he required to complete a building that had stopped short in 1870. But the mini-vogue among writers (or is it among publishers?) for endings to fictions that their authors left unfinished during the 19th century has not thrown up a single modern-dress production.

In this respect, the arts have swopped places. During most of Dicken's mature lifetime it was architecture that versed itself in pastiche and would scarcely venture out except under the veil and justification of some 'historical' style. The novelists, by contrast, had the nerve of the devil. On the strength of nothing less could they have committed themselves to serial publication in the nerve-stretching form it then took.

In his contract for *Drood* Dickens for the first time had a clause inserted providing for arbitration on how much of the up-front money (£7,500 to cover the first 25,000 copies) should be repaid 'if the said Charles Dickens shall die' or be otherwise incapacitated 'during the composition of the said work'. (Presumably nothing had, in fact, to be repaid, since John Forster recorded that 50,000 copies were sold 'while the author yet lived'.) The clause shews that Dickens knew he might be dying, but it is also witness to his splendid confidence that nothing short of death or a stroke could stop him composing the intended dozen monthly numbers.

The more pleasurable suspense that serial publication generated in the consumers (except Queen Victoria, who

41

didn't take up Dickens's offer to disclose *Drood* to her earlier than to her subjects) has now passed to television, leaving to novelists the peace of mind and the diffidence that come from knowing that thousands of readers are *not* hanging on your next instalment.

In the event, Dickens wrote six numbers. The last was two pages short — the second time during *Drood*, that he was failed by the as it were 'ring sense' he had by then reliably cultivated for writing to an exact length. Leon Garfield has opted for the diffident method of completion and has produced an honourable and, where style is concerned, mainly plausible fake. Perhaps at the dictate of publishing economics, he falls far shorter than Dickens did. To fulfil Dickens's design, he should have supplied the same amount of text (equal to six numbers) as Dickens did. But he runs (in the format of this edition) only to 122 pages, whereas Dickens occupies 201.

The outright blots in the Garfield text consist of two howlers in syntax: 'His thoughts were still partly with Rosa, and with she of whom Rosa was an ever-present reminder' and 'And Rosa, what of she?' Dickens was not an elegant syntactician, but I don't think he would have let his narrative do *that*. Elsewhere Mr Garfield's narrative, in contrast to his dialogue, which is on the awkward side, is a forgery good enough, I should guess, to deceive. Try these four in a blindfold test:

As though he had been called into existence, like a fabulous Familiar, by a magic spell which had failed when required to dismiss him, he stuck tight to Mr Grewgious's stool, although Mr Grewgious's comfort and convenience would manifestly have been advanced by dispossessing him.

Ordinarily this animal — the property of the watchman and known, for sufficient reason, as Snap — was of a voracious, biting disposition; but in Vacation time lapsed into a fly-blown apathy, like the law itself, as if all unlawful appetites were but a source of dreamy speculation.

Once in London, where, as usual, the summer is unseasonably warm, and leaden, as if everyone has breathed out and nobody wants to breathe in, she proceeds . . .

There has been rain this afternoon, and a wintry shudder goes among the little pools on the cracked, uneven flag-stones, and through the giant elm-trees as they shed a gust of tears.

Mr Garfield is better at the manner (his are the middle two quotations above, the first and the fourth being from Dickens's text) than at the plot. We know in advance, from Edward Blishen's Introduction, that he is not going to do anything outrageous. He has not taken space enough to do anything deeply complicated. Above all, he is under the great, restricting disability of the faker: he cannot do anything unDickensian. Dickens, of course, could and well might have done, it being his privilege that, the moment he did it, it would *become* Dickensian.

Diligently Mr Garfield extrapolates from the obvious clues in Dickens's text and from some of what Dickens disclosed to friend (Forster), family and illustrator. (Queen Victoria's incuriosity is a smaller loss than critics think. It is inconceivable that Dickens was offering to write her a précis of each number before he wrote the number itself. He can have been offering only to rush her an advance copy. Had she taken him up on it, we should be no better off.) The Garfield Drood *is* dead, and the murderer the obvious suspect, John (or, to Edwin, Jack) Jasper. Something is made of Helena Landless's aptitude for dressing up and something of 'that great black scarf' which, as Dickens's Jasper pulls it off and loops it round his arm, makes his face 'knitted and stern'. Mr Garfield invents an amusingly lightweight Datchery, who is *not* any of the other dramatis personae in disguise. But when the all-important ring is finally recovered (in the manner Forster said Dickens meant it to be), he has Mr Grewgious give it away to Datchery, which Dickens's Grewgious has invested far too much emotion in it ever to do.

Rightly, Mr Garfield makes nothing of the 'Sapsea fragment', no doubt agreeing with Forster that it was designed for an early, not a later, part of the novel and then discarded by Dickens himself. He takes up Dickens's disclosure to Forster that the story was to end in the condemned cell, that the ring was to come uncorroded through the lime that destroys the corpse, that Helena was to marry Crisparkle and that Neville

Landless was to perish, but he ignores Forster's recollection that Neville was to do so 'in assisting Tartar finally to unmask and seize the murderer'.

His is clearly meant to be a reading version, sparing readers the frustration of being left in mid-air, and also a *giving* version. With a shamelessness that is his most deeply Dickensian stroke, Mr Garfield wrenches his story to a conclusion on another, and happier, Christmas. Like many objects designed as Christmas presents, it falls at best flat and sometimes insultingly light. It scurries through the murder trial in a light comedy tone (and *did* judges actually *put on* the black cap?), managing not a touch of the grand grotesquerie that would have been forced from Dickens by his ambivalence towards both crime and punishment. Neither does the Christmas market discharge the publisher from scholarly obligations. The notorious misprint of 'tower' for 'town', twice over, which makes nonsense of Dickens's opening words, is repeated — a laziness that will merely direct buyers towards the Penguin edition, which will leave them in mid-air but does give Dickens's text as it stands in his manuscript. Apart from the fact that they illustrate moments in the fake as well as the Dickens text and can therefore run all through the volume, Antony Maitland's genteel illustrations have no advantages over the 12 (two to each number) plus frontispiece that Luke Fildes drew to Dickens's instructions, from which they anyway borrow the characters' clothes.

A satisfying completion of *Drood* will have to await a writer who can match Dickens's confidence by a confidence on his own part of having understood not just Dickens's style but Dickens's mind. The use of modern language might help, by forcing the writer to decide what he thinks structural and what decorative in Dickens's text. Pastiche can fudge it by using an idiom as ambiguous on that point as Dickens's own. The writer destiny has up its sleeve, who cannot be appointed but must messianically recognise himself, will be confident not only that he can provide a plausible solution to the mystery of Edwin Drood but that he has solved the deeper mystery of *The Mystery of Edwin Drood* — namely, what sort of book it was to be: merely, if magnificently, another Dickens novel or a true mystery in the genre classically established by Wilkie

Collins with *The Moonstone*, which Dickens had published two years earlier in *All the Year Round*?

Either answer points to considerable complexity of plot in the second half. Forster's recollection that the story was to concern 'the murder of a nephew by his uncle' seems to leave no doubt that Edwin is killed. Yet Dickens's notes, skeletal and inconclusive though they are (and broken off at the same point in the story as his text), suggest more emphasis on the uncertainty of Drood's fate than he incorporated in the text before he left it. As well as inquiring 'Dead? Or alive?', his preliminary notes include 'The flight of Edwin Drood' and 'Edwin Drood in hiding'. Perhaps the second half was to revive and prolong the uncertainty or perhaps it was to disclose that Drood did in fact stay alive a little longer than the first half implies. His death need not coincide with his disappearance. Three days elapse before Crisparkle finds his watch in the weir. If Jasper's behaviour has alarmed him, he might pass them 'in hiding' and 'in flight'. And indeed, although Dickens reconciles Edwin and Rosa after they have agreed not to marry, his moralism might well keep Edwin alive long enough to visit on him some ironic remorse for having misprized Rosa.

Certainly, complexity in the second half is argued by Dickens's title for the chapter of the Christmas Eve meeting between Jasper, Neville and Edwin, after which Edwin disappears. I do not think he would have called it 'When shall these three meet again?' had he not planned that there should be a meeting again between Jasper, Neville and at least the corpse of Edwin — which may be what is depicted in the bottom centre vignette in the Fildes frontispiece.

Whether or not Dickens was writing a positive whodunit, he was prompted, I think, to experiment with narrative method by the dovetailed first-person narratives, the one filling in the ignorance and bafflement of the others, in *The Moonstone*. Perhaps he contemplated, though momentarily, a transplant of *The Moonstone* method, crude. The 'Sapsea Fragment' consists, like the narratives in *The Moonstone*, of a document written (by Mr Sapsea) in the first person. But what I suspect he was really after is a variation, less mechanical and more psychological, on Collins's ingenuity.

Rereading Dickens's text, I was astonished to notice that its first five chapters are in the present tense. They include Jasper's opening opium dream and his introduction to Deputy's job of stoning the drunken Durdles home. In Chapter Eight, where Neville and Edwin quarrel at the instigation of Jasper and Jasper's drink, the narrative is again in the historic present. So it is in Chapters Twelve (Jasper's night expedition to the tombs and Durdles's 'dream' of Jasper abstracting the key), Fourteen (the crucial 'When shall these three . . . ?') and Nineteen (Jasper's declaration to Rosa). Chapter Twenty-Two opens in the past tense with a round-up of what has happened meanwhile, but quickly moves into the present tense and stays there for Jasper's opium session and Datchery's detection.

Something very near half of Dickens's text (ten chapters out of 22) is written in the historic present. Apart from Chapter Twenty-Two, which comes from a number where there was a mix-up, both in Dickens's notes and in some editions, about the numbering and the division of chapters, each of Dickens's chapters is either wholly in the past or wholly in the present tense. In other books, Dickens uses the present haphazardly, when it strikes him as apt. In *Drood* I think his switches of tense are systematic.

I cannot name an exact significance for each of the present-tense chapters (though I'd like an acknowledgement, please, if some other critic can), and in some cases the significance may be designed to emerge only in the second half. The effect of Wilkie Collins's systematic jigsaw of narratives is that, for instance, Rachel Verinder can actually see Franklin Blake steal the moonstone and yet, of course, really see no such thing, since not only is his motive non-thieving but he is unaware of his own actions, being, unknown to himself, drugged by opium. My hypothesis is that, by a refinement on Collins, Dickens used the present tense in *Drood* for chapters where something is seen to happen and can be vouched for in good faith by the narrative and yet is not what really happens.

It is obvious how this could come about in the present-tense chapters where Jasper is drugged and in those where Edwin, Neville and Durdles are, on their various occasions, drunk (and sometimes, conceivably, drugged as well, by Jasper). Moreover, some double vision of this sort on Jasper's part, a faculty for seeing what happens correctly yet not seeing what really happens, must, I think, be the interpretation of the most important but the most neglected of the clues Dickens gave Forster — namely, that 'the originality' of the story 'was to consist in the review of the murderer's career by himself at the close, when its temptations were to be dwelt upon as if, not he the culprit, but some other man, were the tempted'.

Thus the fears Jasper expresses, even before Edwin disappears, that Neville will do him violence are, I think, though not true to the facts, sincere: he is expressing his own temptation as Neville's. The same is true of his stated conviction, after Edwin's disappearance, that it is Neville who has murdered him. Jasper's double vision has, so to speak, mistaken Neville's infatuation with Rosa for his own, which, as he avows to Rosa, 'is so mad that, had the ties between me and my dear lost boy been one silken thread less strong, I might have swept even him from your side when you favoured him.'

Those silken ties between Jasper and his dear lost nephew are stronger than critics have allowed. The true and desperate madness in Jasper's love for Rosa seems to me to lie in his not being sure which of the betrothed pair, Rosa or Edwin, he is more in love with. Is he tempted to kill Edwin in order to take Rosa for himself, or tempted to keep Edwin for himself (or at least in the family) by killing Rosa — who is, quite rightly, scared of him to the point of running away to Mr Grewgious's custody? In choosing to kill Edwin, a deed he can plausibly see, through his double vision, as done by Neville, Jasper may even seem to himself to make the right choice, since he thereby suppresses the more culpable of his two sexual passions.

The discovery, which makes Jasper faint, of what Forster calls 'the utter needlessness of the murder for its object', since Rosa and Edwin were not going to marry in any case, perhaps reflects Dickens's sense of personal irony in having wounded his family and risked his respectability for the sake of a mistress with whom he was then not happy. The surname of Helena and Neville is interpreted by Mr Garfield when he makes Helena exclaim: 'We are landless; we are homeless!' Yet, apart perhaps from Honeythunder, the names in *Drood* (including Drood itself) are not of such Restoration Comedy transparency, and they have more to do with Dickens's feelings about the people concerned that with those people's natures. Drood is not a person to inspire either brooding or dread. Neither could one guess that Mr Grewgious, that amalgam of *greed*, *screw* and *egregious*, is, besides angular, good. Landless, which was changed in Dickens's notes from 'Heyridge or Heyfort', owes something, I suspect, to the unusual middle name of Dickens's mistress, Ellen Lawless Ternan, and the Lawless itself must, I think, have sounded in Dickens's thoughts as an indictment of his own behaviour on her account. Jasper attributes his own guilt to Neville Landless, whose surname signified for Dickens, I think, both the lawlessness and the outlandishness of Jasper's desires.

Dickens's narrative could never have *stated* Jasper's sexual love for Edwin, but it can and does *shew* it even more explicitly than *Our Mutual Friend* shews the homosexuality of Eugene and Mortimer. Indeed, in *Drood* Dickens makes his point by deliberate contrasts. A disconsolate Neville, touched on the shoulder by Crisparkle, 'took the fortifying hand from his shoulder, and kissed it' — once, and in any case Neville is markedly not English. What Dickens expected of the English he makes clear when Crisparkle is re-united with his rescuer from drowning, Tartar: 'The two shook hands with the greatest heartiness, and then went the wonderful length — for Englishmen — of laying their hands each on the other's shoulders, and looking joyfully each into the other's face.'

Those exceptional incidents throw into conspicuity the very different conduct of the dinner Jasper gives Edwin in Chapter Two, which begins with Jasper watching Edwin arrive and take off his outer clothes with 'a look of hungry, exacting, watchful, and yet devoted affection' and continues with Edwin's flirtatiously bidding Jasper take him in to dinner, in pursuit of which 'the boy', as Edwin now significantly becomes, 'lays a hand on Jasper's shoulder, Jasper cordially and gaily lays a hand on *his* shoulder, and so Marseillaise-wise they go in to dinner' — in the course of which Jasper lays 'an affectionate and laughing touch on the boy's extended hand', and presently suffers one of his glazed spells, after which Edwin 'gently and assiduously tends him', recovers and 'lays a tender hand upon his nephew's shoulder' and then astonishes Edwin by saying he hates his job, provoking Edwin first to bend 'forward in his chair to lay a sympathetic hand on

Jasper's knee', next to the declaration 'you love and trust me, as I love and trust you' and thus to the demand 'Both hands, Jack,' which leads to uncle and nephew each standing 'looking into the other's eyes' and holding (both) hands through five exchanges of dialogue.

It is this chapter that is, I think, destined eventually, through the disclosures of the second half, to make clear to the reader, though not necessarily, given its present-tense narrative, to the participants, why the murder is inevitable. Rosa is one of the participants by proxy, by means of the much-looked-at amateur portrait of her by Edwin that hangs on Jasper's wall. Edwin elects himself victim by flirting with Jasper and yet not telling Jasper that his heart is not truly engaged to Rosa.

I think the same dinner discloses the method and the immediate occasion of the murder. Luke Fildes's recollection (in 1905) was that Dickens had told him the 'secret' that Jasper's 'double necktie' was an indispensable property because Jasper was to strangle Drood with it. So far as I can see, Fildes didn't draw a Jasper with a double necktie. No doubt commentators are right in thinking that Dickens replaced the necktie by 'that great black scarf' which Jasper takes to the crucial Christmas Eve meeting. All the same, Dickens's thoughts must have continued, in parallel, along the necktie groove. At his reconciliation with Rosa, Edwin explains to her: 'with me Jack is always impulsive and hurried, and, I may say, almost womanish.' In the next chapter, before he goes to the Christmas Eve meeting he reflects: 'Dear old Jack! If I were to make an extra crease in my neck-cloth, he would think it worth noticing!'

Both thoughts are foreshadowed at the Chapter Two dinner, where, while Ediwn takes off his topcoat, hat and gloves, Jasper fusses: 'Your feet are not wet? Pull your boots off. Do pull your boots off.' Edwin replies: 'Don't moddley-coddley, there's a good fellow. I like anything better than being moddley-coddleyed.'

Whether the murder was to have taken place during the Christmas Eve storm or on one of the three ensuing winter nights, I am convinced in my literary bones that it was destined to begin as an act of protective tenderness. Originally, perhaps, Jasper was to tighten Edwin's necktie for him against the cold and Dickens replaced that by an indeed more plausible gesture where Jasper wound his own great black scarf round Edwin's throat. Edwin, I think, was to resist being moddley-coddleyed; and only then was Jasper to make an 'impulsive and hurried' decision (designed, however, to refute and suppress all imputations of the 'womanish') to kill him instead.

Lady Morgan's
The Wild Irish Girl

(Introduction to Routledge and Kegan Paul re-publication, 1986.)

Many novels are deplorably bad. *The Wild Irish Girl* is one of a few to be delightfully so.

First published in 1806, it was the author's third novel. Her previous books, including the collection of verse she began with, were not ignored. One of the novels was said to have consoled the former prime minister, William Pitt the younger, during his last illness. Yet it was the *Irish Girl* that made her name — which was at the time Sydney Owenson.

A new literary lioness both in her native Ireland and in England, she was invited to join the household of the Marquis of Abercorn, who had seats in both countries and who, in the pattern of many noblemen of the period, assembled an entourage part way between an extended family and a minor princely court. There she met the marquis's surgeon, Thomas Charles Morgan, a widower of scholarly disposition for whom the Abercorns secured a knighthood. Morgan fell in love with her, and in 1812 she married him at the insistence of Lady Abercorn, who, given that the marriage turned out extremely happy, seems to have understood her protégée better than she herself did.

Miss Owenson was transformed into Lady Morgan. Except when they dodge behind a pseudonym, present-day writers seldom risk changing an already established professional name. Lady Morgan obeyed the more stringent decorum of the reign of George III. For her readers the change must have been virtually painless, because the *Irish Girl* early began, long kept up and passed to much of her other fiction and non-fiction the habit of going into repeated new editions. Under her

51

married name and style she pursued the remaining more than four decades of her busy career. She was awarded, during the premiership of Melbourne, the first pension for services to literature given to a woman. She still holds her niche in biographical dictionaries; and in 1971 she posthumously resumed her publishing habits with the reissue of the bulk of the text of her two books about her travels and encounters in France.

She died in London, where she had set up residence, in 1859. She was born in Dublin in nobody knows which year. *The Dictionary of National Biography* settles for '1783?', finds that she deliberately hid her age and dismisses Croker's date of 1775 as slander, along with his tale that she was born aboard the Dublin packet. John Wilson Croker, reviewer and Tory politician, did indeed belabour her books, for political reasons, from the *Irish Girl* onward, but his mail-boat invention is rather an inspired metaphor of her mid-Irish-Sea condition. She was the daughter (the elder of two) of an English Methodist from Shrewsbury and the Irish comedic actor Robert Owenson.

After her mother's death she attended a Huguenot school near Dublin, where she acquired her fluent French. Her father, whom she adored, became debt-ridden. When he was declared bankrupt, she declared her intention of earning her own living. The high income of Fanny Burney allured her to literature and after a spell of governessing, where her socially useful gifts of ebullience and harp-playing made her the pet of the families she worked for, she plunged into professional writing.

In *The Wild Irish Girl* she undertook a task seemingly wished on her by destiny: the introduction of Ireland to British readers. Despite the ignorance of many present-day academics, who put its genesis a thousand years later than it was, prose fiction in Europe has a more or less continuous history since the second or third century A.D., when Longus added a masterpiece, *Daphnis and Chloe*, to an already highly sophisticated form. The *Irish Girl*, however, has no truck with sophistication and little with the technique of novel-writing. The epistolary convention, which in the course of the eighteenth century Samuel Richardson had used with extreme emotional power and Choderlos de Laclos had made into an ironic gallery where correspondent flashes ironic light on correspondent, is here flattened into a ribbon of first-person narrative chopped into roughly letter lengths. All the letters are from the son of an English peer as he makes his first visit to his father's property in Ireland, and, in transparent token of the author's politically propagandist purpose, they are all to an English M.P. The events are set back to '17--'. I surmise the author was wishing away the Act of Union, which Pitt and Castlereagh put through in 1800 and which she, as an Irish patriot, deplored, although it was an attempt to give economic and political reality to the mystical marriage of the two islands which the end of her novel adumbrates. At the same time, I imagine, she thought that liberal sympathies would be more easily engaged for Irish rebellion if she suggested a date when the help Irish rebels regularly expected, and regularly failed to get, from the French was sought from revolutionary France rather than from the emperor Napoleon.

As he explores Ireland, the hero-narrator is obliged to discard his English prejudices. London's architecture he finds surpassed by Dublin's, English landscape by Irish — a comparison he makes by way of comparing two seventeenth-century painters, Claude Lorrain and the 'superior genius' of Salvator Rosa, thereby presaging that Lady Morgan was to write a famous biography of Rosa.

When he meets and falls in love with his wild Irish girl, the hero finds her, far from wild, polite and patrician. Indeed, though she uses a conventional name on conventional social occasions, she is by birth an Irish princess. She diplomatically disciplines the peasant boys into humane habits. She deploys the author's own skills of singing and playing the harp. And she is, like her author, a thorough pedant. Through her conversation the novel establishes the greater antiquity of the Irish than of the Welsh harp and indeed of most Irish than of most other things. Through thickets of footnotes the author entices readers by plucking on the voguish concerns of the period, classical antiquity, ethnic tradition and lineage. The far from wild princess bears the exotic first name Glorvina, which a footnote explains:

'Glor-bhin (pronounced vin) is literally "sweet voice"'. The name stuck to the author, whose friends addressed her as Glorvina.

The professional world Sydney Owenson knew from childhood on was the theatre. By theatrical habit, I surmise, she began obscuring her age before she was old enough for anyone to care, and it was no doubt by theatrical usage that she published as 'Miss Owenson' instead of (like her contemporary, Jane Austen, for instance) as 'a lady'. Needing to string her nuggets of antiquarianism on a plot, she again borrowed from the theatre. From time to time she freezes the action on a visually impressive tableau such as might close a scene. The hero learns of the seeming failure of his love-suit by overhearing an aside spoken by Glorvina. When he dashes into the final tableau, the resolution of the story is achieved by the device Aristotle's *Poetics* calls the 'discovery', wherein one character (plus the audience) discovers the true identity of another. Aristotle analyses its use in ancient Greek tragedies like Sophocles's *Oedipus the King*. Thence it was transferred to comedy and is most winningly used by Beaumarchais and, in his wake, by Mozart and da Ponte in *Le Nozze di Figaro*. It may have been from the last station on its journey, popular melodrama, that Sydney Owenson borrowed it for her *Irish Girl*, where the disclosure of the true identity of the hero's rival is unlikely deeply to surprise readers, because, like a careless plotter of detective stories, she has failed to strew her book with potential suspects.

She collected Irish tunes and published them with words of her own, an example said to have been followed in 1807–8 by Sir James Stevenson, as music arranger, and Sydney Owenson's friend and compatriot Thomas Moore, as poet, in their still often poignant *Irish Melodies*. In 1807 the Theatre Royal in Dublin put on a comic opera by Miss Owenson, and on the author's benefit night the women of the Lord Lieutenant's retinue wore gold Irish bodkins of the kind she ascribes to her wild Irish heroine. Her essential talent, I think, and the one that still scents her most famous book is that of a performer and an inspirer of performances, a talent that is fifty per cent courage.

The wing of great literature brushed her more than once. In

1821 Byron wrote to their friend in common, Thomas Moore, bidding him convey to her Byron's approval of her book about Italy, which he called 'fearless'. Anthony Trollope, who worked for the Post Office in Ireland, and who surely modelled the title of his early Irish novel, *The Kellys and the O'Kellys*, on Lady Morgan's *The O'Briens and the O'Flaherties*, published one of his greatest novels, *Castle Richmond*, which is also set in Ireland, in the year after Lady Morgan's death. He must have had her in mind when he plaited into the authorial discourse of his story a lament that Irish novels, once popular, are now 'drugs in the market'. During her lifetime, another English novelist, one with an Irish wife, commemorated Lady Morgan's fame in his greatest novel. *Vanity Fair* is an historical novel. The Battle of Waterloo which constitutes its climax was fought when Thackeray was three. With his perfect-pitch historical novelist's ear, Thackeray gives the marriage-hungry sister of the Irish wife of the Irish Major O'Dowd the name Glorvina. Thackeray is a novelist Homeric enough to nod. I notice that when he brings her back towards the end of the book he muddles her into the sister not, now, of the wife but of the husband and distorts her surname accordingly. But Glorvina she remains.

The original Glorvina did not charm Jane Austen. In January 1809 Jane Austen reported by letter to her sister: 'We have got *Ida of Athens* by Miss Owenson . . . We have only read the Preface yet; but her Irish Girl does not make me expect much. — If the warmth of her Language could affect the Body it might be worth reading in this weather.' Five years later Jane Austen published *Mansfield Park*, a novel of triumphant technique whose subject-matter is morality and charm. Henry Crawford and his sister Mary exercise as compelling a charm as Jane Austen, a specialist in the matter, ever created; it is only the action of the book that exposes them as superficial and rubbishy. I suspect that the book's judgment on them echoes Jane Austen's on Lady Morgan as a writer. I have nothing but intuition to vouch for my speculation, but I believe it was thanks to the accomplishment shared by the Wild Irish Glorvina and her author that the instrument on which Mary Crawford displays her seductive and socially destructive charm is the harp.

The Eye of a Penholder

(*Listener. 1972;* Glory, *by Vladimir Nabokov, Weidenfeld*)

Nabokov's career in the English-reading world is a paradigm of that world's mismanagement of literature. In 1948 *The Real Life of Sebastian Knight* had been on the English market for three years but had done so little trade that remaindered copies were being sold off at half-a-crown. I bought one at the prompting not of critics or dons, none of whom, apparently, had noticed it, but of a fellow-undergraduate. He began by taking a simple fancy to the Russianness of the author's name (which we pronounced VlAdimir NAbokov) but then, with a percipience to which I vow perennial thanks, advised me that the book was a masterpiece.

So it is now widely acknowledged to be — as well as, even on Nabokov's scale, a mastertease: the purported biography of Sebastian Knight (an Anglo-Russian writer one of whose unfulfilled intentions is to write the biography of a fictitious person) by his half-brother, whose narrative ends: 'I am Sebastian, or Sebastian is I, or perhaps we both are someone whom neither of us knows.'

The relation of Sebastian's 'real life' to the author's was plainly more teasing still. But my copy had been divested, before I bought it, of its jacket. Not a scrap of external information was to be had. To me, and to my father, John Brophy, who pursued the enquiry in print, Nabokov remained a mystery for a decade.

In 1958 and 1959, in the US and Britain respectively, artistic justice was suddenly accorded to Nabokov — for the totally non-artistic reason that the theme of *Lolita* coincided with a tiny thaw in Anglo-American puritanism. Fame released information that made clear how belated that fame was. Nabokov had been a master of English prose since 1941, the publication year in the US of *Sebastian Knight*, which was his tenth novel but the first he had written in English. Since *Lolita*, Nabokov has been public, publicly displaying towards the literary and academic establishment an irony by which it is no doubt as baffled as it is hurt. The literary circles which let *Sebastian Knight* go unremarked and remaindered have now been opened to the whole of Nabokov's amphisbaenic oeuvre: his post-*Sebastian Knight* novels in English; and the authorised translations (into North American) of the remaining eight (one translation had been published before *Lolita*) of his pre-*Sebastian Knight* novels in Russian, of which *Glory* is the last to be issued.

Fame was accompanied by normative rumours, which fell disappointingly on an English ear, that the now celebrated author must be called VladImir NabOkov. English tongues cast the stress backwards on Russian names in deference, I believe, to their exoticism. A stress on the penultimate syllable sounds more Mediterranean: Slavic accents must seem more remote. (NabOkov, however, can be rescued for exoticism: actually by its Mediterranean ring. It is surely the Russian for what Italian renders as NabUcco and English as Nebuchadnezzar?). This tendency on the part of English tongues is not, of course, lost on Nabokov's unexcelled and polyglot sensibility to proper names. 'From the garden,' says a passage in *Glory*, 'two feminine voices called Gruzinov's name with the first syllable accented instead of the second. He looked out. The two English girls wanted him to come and have ice cream.'

It is the polyglot and, in this case, comic poetry of proper names that opens *Glory*: 'Funny as it may seem, Martin's grandfather Edelweiss was a Swiss.' The hero of *Glory* has inherited this surname, and it establishes him as a Noble White (Russian) — and also, perhaps by a botany of opposites, as the whiter side of Nabokov, whose preface describes Martin as 'nicer than I' and one of whose pseudonyms (according to Andrew Field) is Vivian Darkbloom. The hero of *Glory* is Martin by, I surmise, ornithological borrowing: he is a natural migrant. His pre-Revolutionary Russian childhood is passed under the presidency of his mother's anglophilia ('she would discuss eloquently such topics as Boy Scouts or Kipling'), his own infatuation with *wagon-lit* travel to Biarritz (that unFrenchly named epitome of Edwardian internationalism whose essence is in fact much better preserved, nowadays, at Bournemouth), and the water colour above his bed of a path through a wood, which invites him to adventure on the model not of a Russian hero but of one of King Arthur's knights, 'perchance a nephew of Sir Tristram's?'

If Malory is right, a nephew (in the full sense) of Sir Tristram must be a non-being. Sir Tristram had no full siblings. However, he had a half-brother — like Sebastian Knight, to whom Martin Edelweiss is linked verbally by his knight-errantry and, in plot, by their both going (like Nabokov himself) to Cambridge. Nabokov's preface forbids readers to compare *Glory* with Nabokov's autobiography. But its reference to a chess problem where the Queen impedes 'one of White's Knights' hints àt a merger between the 'white' of Edelweiss and the Knight who is Sebastian. *Glory* and *Sebastian Knight* are pendants, and both narratives proceed by a series of knight's moves insofar as they often take two steps obliquely for every one that is straightforward.

The Revolution at first merely abets Martin's taste for travel. He and his mother make a leisurely escape, via Athens and Martin's first love affair, to comfortable exile in Switzerland. The narrative, which is more knowledgeable than Martin's consciousness, moves by small side-steps along the route of its, not his, associations. Martin experiences but doesn't understand a suicidal temptation to fall off a Swiss mountain. The narrative's small shifts are in process of turning him completely about. Where his romanticism finally points is back to Russia. He crosses the border illegally, and disappears: down, spiritually, the forest path whose picture presided over his childhood.

His sacrifice, which incidentially does no good to anyone, is pure. It is neither political nor practical. A political émigré (the mis-stressed Gruzinov) from whom he seeks practical hints merely teases him with invented places on the map: Carnagore and Torturovka (Nabokovian anti-Bolshevisms) and 'a very dense wood, called Rogozhin' — which I take for one of

Nabokov's anti-Dostoyevskisms, Rogozhin being the murderer in *The Idiot*.

The preface includes another of Nabokov's customary conceits, his promotion of Freud by what may indeed be the most telling method in a resistant world, namely a blatantly irrational disparagement. Sketching the psycho-analytical skeleton of *Glory*, he remarks that it would be discerned by 'only a blatant saphead'.

From the moment the narrative's impetus turns the migrant towards home, it slackens. The Cambridge scenes, which resemble E. M. Forster at his most *Boy's Own Paper* and include a fight between Martin and his best friend which renders them even better friends, have the flat unreality that usually comes from an author's knowing by experience (instead of imagining) what he is writing about. Perhaps some ironic distance has been lost in translation. Certainly, the stiffness is not eased by North-Americanisms that create impossibilities of dialogue, causing, for instance, an English undergraduate in the early Twenties to say 'You ought to wash up' when (it is after that fight) he means 'You ought to wash.'

Probably, however, the end is diminished by the nature of the excellence of the beginning. Martin had to be a third-person hero, so that he could vanish, and the preface boasts that Nabokov is not so far identified with him as to have made him an artist. But the Russia and childhood from which he is exiled are created by Nabokov's narrative, which is the work of an artist. Impossible to credit the tension that pulls Martin home when the narrative has perfect, sensuous recall. The early chapters of *Glory* are excitingly and movingly beautiful, a restoration of the reader to the childhood immediacy of experience from which we are all exiles, a magic succession of images like (and like that visible in) the penholder that Martin leaves behind in the compartment when, on the way home from Biarritz via Berlin, his family changes trains at the frontier: 'the penholder with the tiny glass lens, in which, when held up to your eye, a mother-of-pearl and blue landscape would flash into being'.

Nabokov published *Glory* in Russian in Paris in 1932. 'Exploit', he explains, is a more direct translation of its Russian title, discarded, however, lest it be read as a verb instead of a noun. Perhaps in the choice of *Glory* there is a sense of answering, not necessarily antagonistically, the title of the still too little praised novel on themes historically similar which William Gerhardie published in 1922, that novel that exists as wholly in the spaces between people as *Glory* does in the sensuous essence of objects, *Futility*.

He/She/Hesh

(LRB, 1982; Handbook of Non-Sexist Writing *by Casey Miller and Kate Swift, Women's Press)*

'Ah, Jane Austen! He is such a great novelist!' That was said to me by a Hungarian émigré, who, when I mildly queried the 'he', explained: 'I find those English pronouns tiresome. We don't have them in Hungarian.' Thus I stumbled on the fact, which I report now in Mario Pei's words (and on his authority, since mine doesn't rise to vouching for a syllable of Hungarian), that 'in Hungarian the same word means "he", "she", "it"'.

Unless things have changed since I was there in 1973, the trams in Budapest are driven by women. Otherwise, Hungary is not a discernible jot more sex-egalitarian than Britain or the USA.

And that conclusively pulls the rug out from under Casey Miller's and Kate Swift's *Handbook of Non-Sexist Writing.* Centuries of being unable to differentiate 'he' from 'she' have not made Hungarians non-sexist. There is not the smallest reason to expect that Britons and residents of the USA will turn non-sexist overnight should Ms Miller and Ms Swift succeed in persuading the 'writers, editors and speakers' for whom their book is confusedly designed (why do speakers need a handbook of writing?) to scrap the 'he' in sentences like 'Anyone who converses with émigré Hungarians will soon find that he is bewildered by their pronouns' and replace it by 'he or she' or one of the other formulae that carry Miller-Swift approval.

Given that it has no hope of reforming society, there is no useful point in the enterprise. Results it may well have, but bad ones. The trouble most Britons experience is not in telling a masculine 'he' from a generic 'he' but in telling 'he' from 'him' ('He said it was to be kept between he and I'). Rapped by pedants and yet subjected to teachers who refuse to (or can't) divulge the rules, chivvied into euphemisms (which often render attractive words unusable — if women do suffer a linguistic injustice, it is that they can no longer make their toilet) but derided for genteelism when they adopt them, warned *de haut en bas* that even old and seemingly innocuous words like 'mirror' may bear the stigma 'non-U', the citizens have come to apprehend their native language as a collection of dangerous taboo objects and are losing all confidence about wielding it. By adding to the areas of taboo, Ms Miller, Ms Swift and their numerous like can only speed the national degeneration into inarticulacy. Having lost the thread of syntax, Britain is becoming a linguistic desolation, imaged, I sometimes feel, in the desolate Southern Region of the railways, where even the euphemisms are now surreally dilapidated and you can look into the corridor and see four shut doors bearing the label 'TO LET'.

Mss M & S are prepared to sanction 'he or she', a phrase they claim has 'made a come-back' despite is clumsiness when it has to be repeated, but what they really applaud is the replacement of 'he is' by 'they are'. The use of 'they' and 'their' as singulars, as in 'Anyone using the beach after 5 pm does so at their own risk' (one of the examples M & S give with applause), clearly delights something in them. But anyone who tried to put a name to it would do so at his, her or their peril. One of the gobbets M & S quote and savage is the remark, which they ascribe to 'a book reviewer', that H. G. Wells can 'exert his magnetism on the small boy in all of us'.

The 'solution' M & S propose in that instance is to replace 'small boy' by 'child'. Most of their 'solutions' have the same depressive effect of sucking the imaginative content out of material that can ill spare it. 'Her craftsmanship was hailed as outstanding' is one of the examples that they have made up (which they differentiate from their authentic quotations) and then re-write. If re-writing is going, I think the cliché at the end of the sentence could do with some, but it is the 'craftsmanship' that excites M & S to disapproval. This, they suggest, should be replaced by what they call a synonyn, 'craft skill'. I doubt if that is a complete synonym and it certainly isn't idiomatic. M & S want to throw away a pleasing word and, at the same time, some of the advantage that English derives from linking its possessive adjective to the possessor instead of the possessed, with the result that English can give new information (his table or her table) where in Italian *la sua tavola* is condemned to giving you, twice over, the anyway erroneous information that the table is female. M & S have persuaded themselves that the *man* component in 'craftsmanship' excludes women. Plainly, however, it doesn't. As their own invented example demonstrates, English can say 'her craftsmanship'.

On the more interesting and quirky subject of bisexual words to which English gives a feminine form, M & S have perversely little to say. I was once driven to public expostulation when a chairman introduced me to an audience as an authoress, but I am aware that Jane Austen, who wasn't Hungarian, wrote of herself as an authoress and that, had the word been ruled out, Samuel Butler could not have turned so succinct a title as 'The Authoress of the Odyssey'.

He couldn't have done the equivalent were the Odyssey a painting. It would be easy to conjecture that we have 'authoress' and 'poetess' (a word that should nowadays provoke fisticuffs in Earls Court Square but that can, in 17th-century parlance, take on the charm of 'shepherdess') because women were early admitted in considerable numbers to literature whereas they were largely kept out of or kept quiet in the visual arts. The conjecture won't, however, work — a fact that might be taken as a pinch of salt with M & S's assertion that the 'vocabulary and grammar' of English often reflect a 'white, Anglo-Saxon, patriarchal' society given to excluding or belittling women. It is true that we have no paintresses, but those yet rarer beings, women who sculpt, go in danger of being called sculptresses.

M & S give a list, extracted from a document compiled by the US Department of Labor, of words that name people's occupations in ways judged to be 'Sex-and-Age-Referent', together with suggested substitutes for them. This includes rewriting 'draftsman' as 'drafter' — which I suppose one can, if one must, understand as describing someone who drafts

63

things. M & S don't, however, say what they would like us to call visual artists who neither paint nor sculpt but draw. Drawers?

As a replacement for 'chairman' M & S, wary of ridicule, propose not 'chairperson' but 'chair'. That may be just passable in their examples, which are all on the lines of 'The new chair will take office at the annual meeting', but I don't think I could have said that I was once introduced as an authoress by a chair. Still, it enriches Edward Lear's 'Said the table to the chair'. M & S seem not to have noticed, however, that English is already working its usual felicitous trick of assigning divergent meanings to doublet forms. A woman who becomes a school governor enters the same professional area as but does not risk being confused with a governess; and although London buses might be said to be more sexist than Budapest trams in that they often have conductresses, Jane Glover is not in danger of being the conductress of an orchestra.

Inevitably, M & S's supposed improvements denature anything that might pass for a joke. I don't think 'We asked the Girl Guides to man the exhibition' is riotously funny, but if destiny forces me to read an account of the village fête I would rather come on that sentence than on its M & S version, 'We asked the Girl Guides to run the exhibition'. Perhaps M & S think it's a mobile exhibition?

To 'those who cannot bring themselves to use *they* in place of *he*' M & S offer further alternatives. They record that the 'anyone . . . he' construction was already being purified in the 19th century by the invention of a sexless singular personal pronoun, *thon*, and that later inventors, who must have been undeterred by *thon*'s lack of success, have variously put forward '*co, E, tey* and *hesh*'. Or one may use *one*, but here the *Handbook* adds a caution: 'In Britain the use of "one" does, however, have specific class implications'.

This I take to be one of the changes made for the British edition by (as Stephanie Dowrick, who made them, puts it in her preface) 'including examples taken from British papers, by occasional rewriting of an American example . . . and by excluding a small amount of material that was very specifically American'. Perhaps those girl guides were originally girl

64

scouts. I also take it that, by 'American', Ms Dowrick does not mean, for instance, Cuban, Brazilian or Bolivian but has done without consulting a handbook of non-imperialist writing.

Another alternative to the singular *they* is, M & S suggest, to recast the whole thing in the plural. They quote and take exception to this sentence from a newspaper: 'Each candidate had to write a description of himself as he thought those who liked, and those who disliked, him would see him.' Knowing from the context that the candidates in question consisted of two men and six women, M & S protest that the sentence they object to excludes the six women — which in context it clearly doesn't, since M & S know of their existence. M & S go ahead all the same and, presumably for the benefit of people who can't read words in context but apprehend them as look-and-say cards in isolation, re-write it as 'The candidates had to write descriptions of themselves as they thought those who liked, and those who disliked, them would see them'. I don't think M & S should have offered to write a handbook for editors while they have obviously mislaid the cross-stitch sampler that hangs on every good editorial wall with the motto 'Perhaps the writer had a reason for putting it like that in the first place'. They haven't noticed that from their re-written version it is no longer possible to be sure whether each candidate had to provide descriptions of one person or of eight.

Having begun their enterprise without ascertaining whether it can reasonably be expected to produce the results they desire, M & S conduct it without much in the way of a coherent concept of the nature of language. They remark that people often resist linguistic change but that changes do happen (of which they give a few arbitrarily chosen instances, chiefly from Old and modern English). These truisms are not enough to establish whether language can and, if so, should be nagged into changing in a programmatic direction. No more is their opening assertion: 'Every language reflects the prejudices of the Society in which it evolved.' Even if you accept the assertion, it does not follow that by changing the language you can change the prejudices. And it is, as a matter of fact, quite some assertion to accept. Are M & S acquainted with 'every language' and (which seems even harder to believe) 'the society in which it evolved'? I am not, but from a much tinier knowledge I should guess that modern English and modern French evolved in fairly similar societies, which indeed at times overlapped and which I imagine had, on matters like monarchy, feudalism, the social position of women, children and non-human animals, chivalry and religion, fairly similar views or 'prejudices'. If M & S are to justify their assertion, they are surely bound to explain either how the same prejudice is reflected both in the French habit of calling a woman and a table alike 'elle' and in the English habit of calling the one 'she' and the other 'it' or in what way French prejudices so differed from English prejudices that they produced a language different in structural type.

M & S's attitude to linguistic change is jolly or, more exactly, jollying along. 'Today', they assure us, 'no one expects a 6-horsepower boat to be pulled by six horses.' Actually, I suspect no one ever did. Surely the word, which the *Shorter Oxford* dates to 1806, was devised to compare mechanical power to beast-of-burden power? What M & S, in their jollity, never mention is that languages are mortal. Certain changes took place, including the development of a slipping clutch about the case endings of Latin nouns, and eventually there emerged the languages of oc and oïl, French, Portuguese, Spanish, and the rest. But it should not be forgotten that Latin dropped dead.

For M & S, a usage is obsolete if some people, unspecified in quantity or quality, don't understand it. Without a nod to the much disputed frontier between popular and educated or between standard and minority usage, they argue that 'man' and 'men' in the generic sense are now misleading and should be scrapped because 'recent studies of college students and school children indicate' that they 'have to a significant degree become inoperative at a subliminal level'. I do not find myself compelled by the argument. To begin with, college students and school children are by definition not completely educated yet. Moreover, I am convinced that, if you put up a notice beside a live wire saying 'A man who touches this wire is likely to lose his life', there is not a woman in the country daft enough to suppose, either subliminally or superliminally, that you are promising her immunity.

Although their leaden literalness of mind forbids them to conceive, whether as metaphor or as psychological perception, that there might be a small boy in us all, women included, M & S rest much of their case against the generic 'he' on the dictum of a small boy. He occurs in an anecdote they quote recorded by 'a teacher': 'I corrected a boy for writing "no one . . . they" instead of "no one . . . he", explaining that "no one" was singular. But he said, "How do you know it was a he?"' Instead of asking why the teacher didn't go on to give the further explanation needed, M & S comment: 'Children can be very logical.' How true, how true. But children can also be ignorant of the resources of English. I daresay the boy in the tale was also unaware of the different senses in which we speak of laws of nature and of the laws of the land, but that is not to say that one of them is obsolete and misleading and should be shot on sight by 'writers, editors and speakers'.

With their tin ear and insensibility to the metaphorical content of language, which is what makes it the vehicle of literature, M & S are inept arbiters of linguistic change. Any minute now they will be forbidding women to read *Du Côté de Chez Swann* or *Treasure Island* on the grounds that there is no small boy in them to whom it could appeal, and likewise warning men off *Alice in Wonderland*. Anyone who has held even a flimsy office (a chairship, perhaps) in the milieu of writers, editors and speakers has probably by now experienced assaults by pressure groups of equal ineptitude trying to nag him into acts of censorship or pledges of self-censorship. The assaults are displacement activities. Writers and editors are considered soft targets and they are attacked because the real targets refuse to give way. When 51 per cent of the chairmanships of banks, industries and cabinet committees are held by women, no one will quibble about addressing the women concerned as 'Mr chairman'. The writers and editors who meantime suffer assault should not give way, and they need experience no crisis of conscience because, if they yielded, they would accomplish nothing whatever for the cause of sex-equality. Their duty is to the language, and to its elasticity and metaphorical power, and the reply they should return to the naggers is 'Co, E, tey and hesh'.

Castle Richmond

(TLS, 1985; symposium on neglected fiction)

Castle Richmond is in paperback print (Dover/Constable). May it inform the (in one of its own phrases) novel-reading world. Despite mini-vogues, chiefly for his least considerable works, and recent scholarly autopsies of the useful but unlovely kind, Trollope still needs hoisting to his proper place up there with Jane Austen and Thackeray as a master of fiction.

Though a 'good long read' and an exciting one, *Castle Richmond* is compact. It is set in Ireland and appeared in 1860, at a time when, as it remarks, Irish novels were out of fashion. With pity and with an analytical eye for the grassroots of politics, Trollope evokes what he calls the 'agony' of the potato famine of 1846–7, which he had witnessed during his Post Office service in Ireland and which forced the hasty repeal of the Corn Laws on the most U-turning of British prime ministers, Sir Robert Peel (a defence of whom Trollope had tossed into the narrative discourse of a novel he published three years before). Against this Trollope sets, in counterpoint, the rivalry between two suitors and between two upperclass families. It imposes a convincing and sympathetic agony of mind on the very young heroine, and on her not-very-old mother it imposes a compact version of the agony of Phèdre.

In Praise of Freud

(LRB, 1982; Psychoanalysis, The Impossible Profession, *by Janet Malcolm, Picador;* Psychoanalytic Psychology of Normal Development, *by Anna Freud)*

'The phenomenon of transference — how we all invent each other according to early blueprints — was Freud's most original and radical discovery. The idea of infant sexuality and of the Oedipus complex can be accepted with a good deal more equanimity than the idea that the most precious and inviolate of entities — personal relations — is actually a messy jangle of misapprehensions, at best an uneasy truce between powerful solitary fantasy systems. Even (or especially) romantic love is fundamentally solitary, and has at its core a profound impersonality. The concept of transference at once destroys faith in personal relations and explains why they are tragic: we cannot know each other.'

Janet Malcolm does not suppose that her distress about a fact will stop its being a fact. Neither is she part of the Freud-processing industry, whose ambition is to pop Freud into the blender and dish up something bland. Hers is a legitimate cry of wounded romanticism. As she utters it, she is adopting one of the methods — indeed, the classical (as well as the romantic) method — whereby humans can snatch pleasure, of a sort, out of distress, namely to discern in the distressing fact the dignity and beauty of tragedy. In token of that aesthetic manoeuvre, the paragraph Ms Malcolm herself constructs about the matter is a pretty good one.

All the same, I suspect that her cry is unjustified and the consolations of tragedy uncalled for. If you truly have accepted the ideas of infantile sexuality and the Oedipus complex, you cannot have much in the way of a just cause to balk at the transference, which represents the continuation of their importance into adult life.

Perhaps the paragraph is hooked on the determinist snag, which can bedevil any hypothesis that attributes causes — or can, at least, appear to, since it is partly a semantic conundrum. 'I wish I were a different person' is in a way an unwishable wish: if it came true, the I who wished it would no longer be there to receive the gratification. Likewise, to wish oneself free of the factors, whatever they are, that determine one's personality, including one's wish to be free of them, is to wish that personality and its wishes out of existence. Ms Malcolm is too sensible to be wishing away the concept, as such, of transference, an abolition that would leave us still blundering about in our Oedipal fog but without even the knowledge that we are doing so. It is presumably the phenomenon itself that she deplores. She seems to imply that, but for transference, we should be able to apprehend one another clearly and love one another for what we are. But if our personalities were not precipitated by our Oedipal experience and formed by it into an apparatus that continues to pursue Oedipal shadows, the result would be that we should not be we, either as individuals or collectively, since we should be a different type of animal.

There seems also to be an implication in the paragraph that there is some method by which our individualities could have been formed that would be more acceptable. But is there? Would it be nicer if we were 'the stars' tennis balls' and our relationships consisted of our collisions as we were 'struck and bandied'? Would being in love be less 'solitary' if it were a spell cast by the capricious intervention of Aphrodite? Would it be less 'impersonal' if the great loves of our lives were dictated by a computer with a facility for spewing random numbers? Should we be more autonomous if we owed our loves and hates not to the Oedipus situation and, by derivation from it, to transference, positive and negative, but to 'something chemical', which, as the narrator of *Brideshead Revisited* remarks, was 'the cant phrase of the time' (the Twenties), 'derived from heaven knows what misconception of popular science' and employed 'to explain the over-mastering hate or love of any two people'? I suspect in passing that that cant

70

phrase may have derived not only from 'popular science' but from scenes like the one the narrator records of under-graduates 'making for the river' carrying what he misnames 'the *Unpleasant Plays* of Bernard Shaw', though in point of pedantic fact it is in *Plays Pleasant*, and specifically in *You Never Can Tell* (1897), that Valentine (who may, as a dentist, represent both popular and unpopular science) declares to Gloria Clandon: 'You cant deny that there is such a thing as chemical affinity . . . Well, youre attracting me irresistibly. Chemically.'

Transference, not in its generalised but in its narrow sense of the emotions felt towards the analyst by an analysand (who is not always, of course, a patient but may be a prospective analyst undergoing his 'training analysis') is Ms Malcolm's central theme. Her book, an expansion of an article written for the *New Yorker*, is in effect a conglomerate profile of the New York Psychoanalytic Institute, in which many of the *dramatis personae* appear, like the patients in psychoanalytical case histories, under pseudonyms, including her central figure and mouthpiece for pscyhoanalysis, 'Aaron Green'. He is endowed with an appearance ('he looks Jewish'), an age (at 46, he is one of the 'younger members'), clothes (grey flannel trousers and a herringbone jacket) and an idiosyncrasy ('the desire to be a beautiful woman'), but even so I think he may be a composite portrait, especially since he tells Ms Malcolm that, after buy-ing his first herringbone jacket early in his career, he noticed that 'everyone at the New York psychoanalytic wears this kind of jacket'.

The journalist's habit of seeking his story where he senses conflict and personal emotion might anyway have led Ms Malcolm to concentrate her enquiries on the transference, but psychoanalysis had already done that for her. The trans-ference re-animates the analysand's original Oedipal relation-ship, and it is the analysis of the transference that makes the Oedipal experience accessible. An unreconstructed Freudian, Aaron Green 'closes his eyes and groans softly' at the mention of Melanie Klein — which, to me at least, is one of the many sympathetic characteristics that Ms Malcolm gives him. The suckling's relation to the breast (or, as the Kleinians have it, to good breast and bad breast), important though it is, cannot

71

justly displace the Oedipus complex from the centre of the psychic organisation, because it lacks the conflict essential alike to dramatic tragedy, good journalism and the precipitation of a personality. It may seem to the suckling that he is performing an act of cannibalism, but in fact what he does has the mother's consent. It is only when the infant asserts his incestuous wishes that the parents are bound to resist. Civilisation depends on their doing so — and prehistorically arose, if Freud is correct, from their doing so.

The analyst, cast by the transference in the parental rôle, is thereby bound to an 'abstinence' that Ms Malcolm finds near-saintly. Not only must he refrain from falling into the arms the analysand will almost certainly extend. He must deny himself even those polite murmurs of commiseration and agreement by which, in ordinary social life, one establishes oneself in one's interlocutors' eyes as a nice person, because such murmurs might inhibit the analysand from expressing hostility.

As therapy, psychoanalysis can usefully treat only a comparatively small number of types of disturbance, which need careful diagnosis. As theory, it can probably touch with illumination virtually everything except the specific content of the physical sciences. Freud's was one of the supremely commanding minds. If Aristotle, in the *Organon*, codified the syntax of rational thought, it was Freud who discovered the syntax of irrational impulses and their often distorting impact on reason. 'It may rationally be said that every person is mad once in every twenty-four hours', wrote Thomas Paine in the Essay on Dream that constitutes the third part of *The Age of Reason* (of 1794 to 1795). A century later, Freud used reason to interpret the language in which our nightly lunacy expresses itself.

Freud's accounts of his own and his patients' dreams lack nothing except circumstantial detail. Significant detail is, of course, abundant. Everything the dreamer says about the room he dreamed he was entering may be valuable secondary elaboration or association that can lead to the meaning of the dream. But in the nature of psychoanalysis the details are not valuable for their own sake, as they would be to a novelist and often are to the dreamer. Ms Malcolm's book restores the insignificant details to psychoanalysis or, at least, its milieu, at least in New York. Her analysts have not only clothes but consulting rooms furnished in certain styles. She reports what they gossip about (the rare occasions when an analyst has broken the abstinence rule) and how they spend their spare time (chiefly with fellow analysts). Her book is entertaining and readable and also well-researched, citing and quoting many of Freud's own books and pursuing a persuasive psychoanalytical hypothesis of Ms Malcolm's own about why Freud picked a particular pseudonym to cloak a particular patient. It reads like a novel by a very, very intellectually classy Arthur Hailey.

Janet Malcolm credits her 'Aaron Green' with a sympathetic line in self-satire when he recounts that his training analysis was conducted by an analyst who had himself been analysed by Ferenczi, who had been analysed by Freud: 'I could thus trace my analytic lineage back to Freud. You smile, and you should. It's a preposterous notion. It's the most primitive kind of family romance — my parents are aristocrats, I'm descended from royalty, all that sort of stuff.' At first glance you might suspect the International Psycho-Analytic Library (which has modified its jackets from fern to lime green but not yet taken up herringbone) of deference to lineage in adding to its collection of Anna Freud's writings an eighth volume containing papers written between 1970 and 1980. Several, it's true, are short and a few slight. Yet even when delivering a sliver of personal reminiscence in the constraining circumstances of a memorial meeting or the re-issue of someone else's book, Anna Freud seems to make an honourable point of never saying nothing. In addition to the slivers, there are substantial discussions of child analysis, from the point of view of both technique and theory, a paper on training analysis which won't be read by everyone who reads Ms Malcolm's book but should be, a longish 'study guide to Freud's writings' that is the definitive answer to the beginner's question about where to begin, and a succinct study of aggression that lends theoretical and clinical support to Freud's recognition, still not universally endorsed by Freudians, of an independent instinctual Thanatos — a recognition that would be my candidate for, in Ms Malcolm's words, 'Freud's most original and radical discovery', because it perceives that the most remarkable thing about life as a biological phenomenon is death.

H. E. Mingway

(Symposium contribution, Dictionary of Literary Biography Yearbook, 1985, Bruccoli-Clark, S.C., USA)

A culture that should have learnt better from Ambrose Bierce, Henry James, Edith Wharton, Scott Fitzgerald and Dashiell Hammett let itself be conned by Ernest Hemingway.

He took up slushy romances and he re-wrote their content in baby syntax like this and he pretended that tormenting and killing animals who are no threat to you was a brave and somehow a mystical thing to do and he perhaps supposed that pretending was the same as imagination and he also pretended that it was laudable to read with your finger running along beneath the line and after a while that pretence became true of him and he misread the first three letters of his own surname and he thought that his name said 'he-man'.

His chum Gertrude Stein was three times the writer as well as twice the man.

In Praise of Lodge and Shakespeare

(1978, televised introduction to As You Like It, *BBC)*

As You Like It is a play I've loved virtually all my life, but it was only recently that I realised that it isn't what the current Copyright Act would call an 'original work'. This is not a great feat of literary detection on my part. Almost all Shakespeare's plays have sources of some kind and any school text will tell you that the source of *As You Like It* is a novel called *Rosalynde* by Shakespeare's contemporary, Thomas Lodge. However, very few people bother actually to read Lodge's novel, and that's a pity, because it is a highly interesting novel in its own right — rather eccentric, deeply charming, very shrewd about psychology, very lively, very well written — and the moment you do read it you realise that it is very much more than just a source for *As You Like It*. *As You Like It* is, in fact, an absolutely straightforward dramatised version of Lodge's *Rosalynde*.

The novel was first published in 1590 and it evidently had a considerable success. It ran to three editions within the next decade. That, presumably, made it worthwhile for someone to cash in on it. It's notable that Shakespeare didn't change the name of the heroine, which the novel had made famous by its title. He kept the name Rosalind, though not for his title. It was eight or nine years after the novel was published, in 1598 or 1599 (no one knows for sure which), that the dramatised version appeared on the stage, under the title *As You Like It*.

Shakespeare did change the names of several of the other characters, but he didn't change the characters themselves or — which is more important — the relationships between them. He cut down the time spanned by the novel, because a novel has more room to stretch than a play has. But on the

76

whole he made fewer changes than a modern writer might if he were adapting a modern novel for the theatre or for television.

Having stayed with Lodge in all the big things, relationships, characters, plot and sequence, Shakespeare often chose to say with him down to smallish detail. For example, here are some details as they occur in Lodge:

> After his repast he fell in a dead sleep. As thus he lay, a hungry lion came hunting down the edge of the grove for prey, and espying Saladyne, began to seize upon him. But seeing he lay still without any motion, he left to touch him, for that lions hate to prey on dead carcasses, and yet desirous to have some food, the lion lay down and watched to see if he would stir. While, thus, Saladyne slept secure, fortune . . . brought it so to pass that Rosader . . . came . . . pacing down by the grove with a boarspear in his hand in great haste. He spied where a man lay asleep and a lion fast by him. Amazed at this sight, as he stood gazing, his nose on the sudden bled, which made him conjecture it was some friend of his. Whereupon drawing more nigh, he might easily discern his visage, and perceived by his physiognomy that it was his brother Saladyne.

When Shakespeare came to dramatise this minor episode, he got rid of the nose bleed and inserted a snake. Otherwise he changed very little. He kept even the detail that lions won't eat carrion:

> A wretched ragged man, o'ergrown with hair,
> Lay sleeping on his back. About his neck
> A green and gilded snake had wreath'd itself,
> Who with her head nimble in threats approach'd
> The opening of his mouth; but suddenly,
> Seeing Orlando, it unlink'd itself,
> And with indented glides did slip away
> Into a bush; under which bush's shade
> A lioness, with udders all drawn dry,
> Lay couching, head on ground, with catlike watch,
> When that the sleeping man should stir; for 'tis
> The royal disposition of that beast
> To prey on nothing that doth seem as dead.
> This seen, Orlando did approach the man,
> And found it was his brother, his elder brother.

Lodge's novel and Shakespeare's play are set in France. One thread concerns a king of France who is driven out of his court by his usurping brother. Shakespeare demotes this pair of brothers from kings of France to dukes of an unnamed part of France. The exiled king or duke is eventually followed into exile by his daughter Rosalind, but not before she has fallen in love with another ill-used brother, who has been driven out of his inheritance by his elder brother and who also goes into voluntary exile.

The place where all these exiles take refuge and where the threads of the story are woven is what Lodge and Shakespeare called the Forest of Arden and what we should call, now that it's no longer fashionable to anglicise French names, the Ardennes. The ups and downs of fortune, which have turned these people into exiles, give them all the opportunity to reflect on blind fortune — or random chance, as we would probably call it — and this gives the play its fashionable philosophical tone; and the fact that they have all taken refuge in the forest puts the play slap in the middle of another high fashion of the Renaissance, which remained in high fashion deep into the eighteenth century, the fashion for the pastoral.

Although a pastor is, literally, a shepherd who puts his sheep out to pasture, I can assure anyone who feels, as I do, that the countryside is highly over-rated that the pastoral fashion has remarkably little to do with real countryside or with real sheep-rearing. When they arrive in the forest Rosalind and Celia do buy a sheep farm, but even in Lodge, who has more room, they are only moderately serious about working it. In Shakespeare, it is obviously left to run itself. The object of the pastoral was not really to draw any morals from nature. It was to re-create the literature of the ancient world — in particular, the pastoral poems, the dialogues mainly between shepherds, which Theocritus wrote in Greek in the third century B.C. and Virgil imitated in Latin a couple of centuries later.

If you bought a pastoral novel or went to see a pastoral play, you knew pretty much what you were going to get, just as nowadays you know pretty much what you're going to get if you buy a thriller. You were going to get shepherds, with Greek or Latinised names like Sylvius, Corin, Lycidas,

Damon, and shepherdesses called things like Phoebe and Corinna. The point of the whole piece was going to be that people were going to fall desperately in love, and you knew also that you'd get large quantities of lyric verse. The idea that shepherds were poets may have begun, I think, from the thought that shepherds piped to their flocks and perhaps, having piped a tune, they then set words to the tune. However it arose, one of the rules of the pastoral convention is that shepherds are poets. In Shakespeare's dramatised version, only one of the characters, Orlando, has the actual verse-writing mania. No doubt he picks it up from the pastoral setting like an infection when he arrives in the forest. Orlando's verses, incidentally, are all bad. However, the entire play is punctuated by songs, which seem to leave their echo in the forest, creating patches of mood, like mist, in the play.

The shepherds in Theocritus and Virgil often fall passionately in love with shepherdesses and they also quite often fall passionately in love with shepherds. The same is probably true of the cowboys in the modern western, which is a diluted descendant of the pastoral.

This tradition of the pastoral made it a particularly apt mode for Lodge and for Shakespeare in Lodge's tracks to set their story in. When the girl cousins and best friends, Rosalind and Celia, run away to the Forest of Arden, Rosalind — and it is Rosalind rather than Celia because, as she explains, she is the taller of the two — dresses up as a boy. As you'd expect, given that the novel is knee-deep in classical allusions and the play is at least ankle-deep, some having been cut out to make it more easily assimilable in the theatre, the name which Rosalind chooses for herself while she'd disguised as a boy is Ganymede, the name of the page whom Zeus, king of the gods, fell in love with.

Lodge plays with grammar. He calls Rosalynde 'Ganymede', 'he' and 'she' within a single sentence. Shakespeare, of course, had an extra decorative dimension to play with, because women didn't appear as actors on the English stage for another generation, and therefore all the parts in *As You Like It* were taken by men. Rosalind was that old favourite of the English theatre, a drag act, from the word go, and when she disguises herself as a boy she goes into double drag; and at the same time a very delicate and charming air of sexual ambiguity comes over the story. Phoebe falls in love with Ganymede, but of course Ganymede doesn't really exist. Is she in fact in love with Rosalind? Orlando constitutes an even greater dilemma. He believes that, if he pretends that Ganymede (as he thinks he is) is his Rosalind and he woos him, he will be cured of his love for her; and so he does woo the boy and in the process falls deeper and deeper in love with the woman. Or *is* it with the woman? Is it in fact with the boy?

Rosalind:	But come, now I will be your Rosalind in a more coming-on dispostion; and ask me what you will, I will grant it.
Orlando:	Then love me, Rosalind.
Rosalind:	Yes, faith, will I, Fridays and Saturdays, and all.
Orlando:	And wilt thou have me?
Rosalind:	Ay, and twenty such.
Orlando:	What sayest thou?
Rosalind:	Are you not good?
Orlando:	I hope so.
Rosalind:	Why then, can one desire too much of a good thing? Come, sister, you shall be the priest and marry us. Give my your hand, Orlando. What do you say, sister?
Orlando:	Pray thee, marry us.
Celia:	I cannot say the words.
Rosalind:	You must begin, 'Will you, Orlando' —
Celia:	Go to. Will you, Orlando, have to wife this Rosalind?
Orlando:	I will.
Rosalind:	Ay, but when?
Orlando:	Why, now, as fast as she can marry us.
Rosalind:	Then you must say 'I take thee, Rosalind, for wife'.
Orlando:	I take thee, Rosalind, for wife.

If I ask myself what makes *As You Like It* so moving, I locate the answer in two elements that Shakespeare dramatised quite brilliantly from Lodge's novel: the erotic love between Rosalind and Orlando and, slightly less obviously, the non-erotic love between Rosalind and Celia. The dialogue that expresses these relationships may not be positively witty in the sense that you could go through it taking out bits for an anthology of aphorisms, but it is witty in tone, witty in rhythm — and its tone is, of course, the tone of flirtation. Rosalind and Celia are limbering up their flirtatiousness on one another.

If I go on to ask myself how Shakespeare achieved this technically, the answer is one that I think is rather surprising or would be surprising if you knew only his other comedies. He does it in prose:

Celia: Trow you who hath done this?

Rosalind: Is it a man?

Celia: And a chain that you once wore, about his neck. Change you colour?

Rosalind: I prithee, who?

Celia: O Lord, Lord! It is a hard matter for friends to meet; but mountains may be removed with earthquakes, and so encounter.

Rosalind: Nay, but who is it?

Celia: Is it possible?

Rosalind: Nay, I prithee now with most petitionary vehemence, tell me who it is.

Celia: O wonderful, wonderful, and most wonderful wonderful, and yet again wonderful, and after that, out of all whooping!

Rosalind: Good my complexion! Dost thou think, though I am caparison'd like a man, I have a doublet and hose in my disposition? One inch of delay more is a South Sea of discovery. I prithee tell me who is it quickly, and speak space. I prithee take the cork out of thy mouth that I may drink thy tidings.

Celia: So you may put a man in your belly.

Even if you discount the superstitions about the innocence and simplicity of life in the country, there is a way in which

81

shepherds can truly be said to be innocent. This doesn't apply to cowboys, incidentally. Shepherds are innocent of bloodguilt. Human beings don't always choose to do so but it is possible to live on reasonably fair terms with a flock of sheep. You can deprive the sheep of their wool, which they are quite glad to be rid of, and not deprive them of their lives. One of the changes that Shakespeare did make in dramatising Lodge's novel was to shift the economy from sheepminding to hunting. His exiled courtiers in the forest kill the deer. And in this way he darkens the sunny landscape that he found in Lodge.

All the same, through that imperfect windy instrument, Jaques, Shakespeare does allow the point of view of the deer to be stated. It's Jaques who has pointed out to his fellow courtiers in exile that wounded deer weep, which is a matter of fact, incidentally, not a matter of folklore as is usually thought. Jaques makes his entrance, asking the telling question 'Which is he that killed the deer?', a question in which he, as well as looking for someone to congratulate on his victory, is also the detective hunting out a killer; and the song that follows — although it does congratulate the killer on his victory — also makes a mockery of him:

Jaques:	Which is he that killed the deer?
Lord:	Sir, it was I.
Jaques:	Let's present him to the Duke, like a Roman conqueror; and it would do well to set the deer's horns upon his head for a branch of victory. Have you no song, forester, for this purpose?
Another Lord:	Sing it; 'tis no matter how it be in tune, so it makes noise enough.
SONG.	What shall he have that kill'd the deer? His leather skin and horns to wear: Then sing him home.

The English-speaking theatre's other grand master of dramatic prose, Bernard Shaw, considered *As You Like It* a 'melodrama', on the grounds that the hero and heroine have no disagreeable qualities. Presumably he missed (or didn't consider disagreeable) the distinct touch of sadism which I discern in Rosalind's personality. He considered that *As You Like It* gives unmixed delight, but he thought this was simply a bid for popularity. He said Shakespeare flung Rosalind at the public with a shout of 'As *you* like it'.

And, of course, it *was* a bid for popularity. It was a bid for the popularity which Lodge's novel had already established with readers. My guess is that, when Shakespeare had finished making his adaptation, he riffled through the pages of Lodge's novel, casting about for a title, and finally he turned back to the beginning and came upon Lodge's preface, which is addressed to 'the gentlemen readers'.

'To be brief, gentlemen', Lodge says, after relating how he wrote the book on a sea voyage when he was taking part in a military expedition, 'room for a soldier and a sailor, that gives you the fruits of his labours that he wrote in the ocean, when every line was wet with a surge, and every humorous passion counterchecked with a storm. If you like it, so . . .'

By the time Shakespeare made his adaptation, the gentlemen readers had already proved that they did indeed like Lodge's novel. It was no longer a question of '*if* you like it', but '*as* you like it'.

Tailoring

(LRB, 1981; Bernard Shaw and the Actresses, *by Margot Peters, Columbus)*

Mozart had a discernible tendency to fall in love with his sopranos, Shaw something little short of a compulsion to fall in love with, first, women who took singing lessons from his mother and then, after he turned dramatist, his actresses. This must be one of the hazards of creating works of art that need executants to perform them. Ordinary lovers are sometimes dismayed to find that their beloved is in effect their own invention, a fantasy they have unwittingly devised to inhabit the attractive externals of some real person; and something similar seems liable to happen in reverse when an artist deliberately invents a *dramatis persona* and designs it, as he goes along, to wear the trappings of a particular executant. It was surely with autobiographical import that Shaw's imagination was seized by the fable of Pygmalion, the sculptor who fell in love with his own creature. When he eventually wrote *Pygmalion*, he designed the rôle of Eliza for Mrs Patrick Campbell. He went to persuade her to take it and, as he reported to Ellen Terry, 'fell head over ears in love with her in thirty seconds'.

Shaw was at the time 55 and Mrs Pat, who, on taking Shaw's hand, performed what he called the 'infamous abandoned trick' of brushing it against her breasts, 47. (She was 49 by the time she 'created' Eliza on the stage.) They set a stern and inspiring example to us all.

Eliza, Shaw told Ellen Terry in 1912, was 'almost as wonderful a fit' for Mrs Pat as Lady Cicely (the rôle he had lovingly designed for her in *Captain Brassbound's Conversion*) for Ellen Terry: 'for I am,' he added, 'a good ladies' tailor, whatever my shortcomings.' Perhaps it is just that the psychological circumstances coincide or perhaps Shaw was alluding to Mozart, his 'master beloved by masters', some of whose letters were known, though a collected edition did not appear until 1914. The 21-year-old Mozart reported to his father in 1778 that he had tried to compose an aria (K.294) for the tenor Anton Raaff, but, deciding it would go better for a soprano, designed it instead 'exactly for' the voice of Aloysia Weber. (Mozart *père* had no difficulty in reading the unwritten information that he was in love with her.) Mozart prefaced his account with the remark 'For I like an aria to fit a singer as perfectly as a well-made suit of clothes.'

From music pupils to actresses was a short step for Shaw's susceptibility. After all, he treated the casts of his plays as if they were his drama pupils, a habit that provoked, as Ms Peters records, mild remonstrance from some established players. Yet his tuition was necessary — precisely because he composed his plays as though they were operas and required actors to approach his lines of dialogue as though they were singers approaching a vocal line. He was trying, he told one actress, 'to do fine counterpoint': in three parts in *Candida*, in seven in what he naturally called 'the finale' of *The Philanderer*. He knew that the emotions in his plays had to create 'new intellectual speech channels' and even perceived that 'for some time these will necessarily appear so strange and artificial that it will be supposed that they are incapable of conveying emotion' — a still current misapprehension which he combated by, again, operatic analogy: 'They said for many years, remember, that Wagner's endless melody was nothing but discord.'

I imagine it was the Vandaleur Lee 'method' of training the singing voice (which, Shaw claimed, preserved his mother's voice 'perfectly until her death at over 80') that Shaw adapted to speech, first training himself as a public speaker, with results to be heard in recordings of his broadcasts, and then training his performers. Shavian drama demands a conductor's view of the strategy (the pacing and dynamics) and a singer's of the tactics: rhythmical phrasing; plosive consonants and pure, melody-carrying vowels; equal values for the two-note 'I am' and 'did not' which he prefers more often than idiom warrants to the naturalistic slurred contractions. Now that his own tuition is vanishing from living memory, the London theatre has lost its grip on Shavian style. It could be recovered more swiftly than, say, the only recently rediscovered knack of performing Monteverdi, since all that is needed is to saturate everyone connected with a Shaw production in performances of the operas of Mozart and Wagner, which are the essential sources (infinitely more than Ibsen) of Shaw's playwright's technique.

Ms Peters is not particularly alert to musical Shaw, but she appreciates him as literature and is in general a relief after the preternatural proportion he has attracted of duds and dunces. She seems to have small impulse to create literature herself. Her points are more correct than telling, and she seldom builds them into an argument. When it is not directly quoting, her book is heavyish going. It is written with surprising barbarism. People decline from invitations and separate with each other. It declines not from but into grammatical monstrosity: 'She had might as well . . .' Ms Peters regularly writes 'titivate' where she means 'titillate'. Yet she quotes Shaw using 'titivate' correctly. (What can she suppose him to be saying when he writes of his secretary's 'titivating herself' in his presence?) Her book is best read as an intelligent though inelegant commentary on Shaw's early and middle letters and plays and on the novels he wrote in the 19th century. Of the short novel he published in 1932 she gets the very title wrong. And poor Henry Arthur Jones must have suffered enough from his name without being transposed into Arthur Henry.

Shaw's near-compulsion was not a fetish. He was capable of loving women who werer neither singers nor actresses. Indeed, he married one of them — who, if Ms Peters has correctly interpreted his reticent account, reversed the conventions of the time by going to bed with him before they were married but not after. Ms Peters is chiefly interested, however, in the actress-manageresses who put Ibsen and Shaw into currency in the English theatre, and the most informative part of her book gives substance to the name of Florence Farr and of Janet Achurch, whose sad and drink-ruined career Shaw had pre-invented in *The Irrational Knot*.

The feminism of the turn of the 19th century found a focus,

if not leadership, in dramatic heroines, whether the New Woman of Ibsen or the merely novelty woman fabricated by Pinero and played by, *par excellence*, Mrs Pat. In this it was comparable to the feminism of the Restoration, which was focused by the English theatre's discovery that it could no longer make do with boys but must have women players, and which was actually prepared to countenance women dramatists too. It was comparable also to 18th-century feminism because that owed much to the runaway international vogue for opera, where skilled women were needed for reasons both dramatic and musical, since the castrato voice, while it might match the register, could not replace the timbre of their voices. The playhouse and the opera house, junctions of Society and Bohemia, made women fashionable, the questions of what and how they thought and felt piquant. Alan Dent's biography of Mrs Patrick Campbell quotes an expression by George Cornwallis-West of the excitement generated: 'people flocked to see a play written by one brilliant woman and produced by another.' He was writing of the year 1909; the playwright was Lady Randolph Churchill, the producer (and principal actress) Mrs Pat. Cornwallis-West married them both.

Public curiosity about women could be satisfied also, though silently, by novels. The standard *opera seria* aria where the heroine declares herself torn between love and duty has a close copy in the heroine's accounts of her feelings in epistolary novels. Independent of performers, novels kept going through the fluctuations in the fashionableness of women in the theatre, and for social reasons they were more likely than plays and operas to be by, as well as partly about, women. Ms Peters may be right in surmising that the £200-a-week Irving paid Ellen Terry in the Nineties 'probably made her, with the exception of the Queen, England's highest-paid woman', but my guess is that, if there is a contestant, she was a novelist. Marie Corelli, for instance, is estimated (in Eileen Bigland's biography) to have been averaging £10,000 a novel by 1901, and she had been writing roughly one a year since 1886.

Shaw's own intrinsic feminism Ms Peters attributes to his being 'the "complete outsider"', whose social position, without money, formal education or power, resembled women's. This is true, though as thousands of men shared the position and weren't feminists, you are still left with an inherent something to reckon with; and I would rather myself place the point of resemblance in his being a complete insider. After his spells in the Dublin land agent's office and with the Bell Telephone Company in England he was a resolute stay-at-home, un-domesticated but deeply domestic, and resentful, after his marriage, even of the travels his wife made him undertake. Ironically, he helped emancipate middle-class women, in-cluding his future wife, whom he employed as secretary, by giving them the dignity (in socialist eyes) of going out to work, but the transaction left him merely an employer in his own home, which every middle-class housewife was at that period, a seemingly capitalist but without capital. I suspect it was his own self-employed homeworker status that misled Shaw into thinking that copyright was a species of property in economic reality as well as by legal fiction, and into supposing that artistic creators are to be analysed as capitalists, collecting royalties on their property as landlords collect rent on theirs, whereas they are in socio-economic fact workers though workers of a special kind since their labour needs no visible raw material but creates something out of, apparently, nothing, rather as energy can create matter.

The hero of *Man and Superman* is given Shaw's intellectual characteristics and passages of his spiritual autobiography but not Shaw's social position. Shaw could not have appended to his name 'M.I.R.C. (Member of the Idle Rich class)'. I think it is the heroine, Shaw's Everywoman, driven by the Life Force to unscrupulous lengths to secure a father and a home for her children and thereby fulfill her biological vocation, who incar-nates the inmost depths of Shaw: a Shaw driven by the Life Force and his vocation to a deliberately childless marriage which he ever afterwards suspected had the unscrupulous pur-pose of providing the necessary home-workplace and financial security for him to give to his masterpiece.

Her condensed narrative cannot substitute for their auto-biographies, biographies of them and, still less, their corres-pondences with Shaw, but Ms Peters makes a good job of Ellen Terry and Mrs Patrick Campbell, who reigned over the English theatre and Shaw's heart like perfect images of Sacred and Profane Love. She might have mentioned that the name Shaw gave his Superman, John Tanner, an anglicised version of Don Juan Tenorio (the 'Don' being translated into 'M.I.R.C.'), was by bizarre chance the name of Mrs Patrick Campbell's father. I think Shaw may have had an unconscious superstitious fatality about names, since, by another bizarre chance, he married someone of the same surname (Townshend) as his first (land agent) employer. And given that she remarks that Mrs Pat could 'play with him like a child in his dream world', she might have made space, among the book's excellent photographs, for Max's two drawings of the pair as they appeared to their respective selves (romping, child-like, hand in hand) and as they appeared to each other (dessicated Shaw shrinking from overpowering and over-hanging Mrs Pat).

Ms Peters makes a good point of Shaw's respect for Irving, who was perhaps Shaw's only worthy antagonist. Shaw never wholly won the tussle for Ellen Terry's heart and professional soul. I have a strong feeling that Irving's nobly sinister appear-ance and his emotional preying on Ellen Terry were, whether knowingly or not, put by his business manager, Bram Stoker, into *Dracula*. No more did Shaw ever wholly entice Ellen Terry from the middlebrow world into the intelligentsia. In her private life she broke every middle-class convention of the period and yet came through with the aura of holiness Homer attributes to the elderly Helen of Troy. To Shaw's announce-ment that he had fallen in love with Beatrice Stella Patrick Campbell, Ellen Terry made the exactly right reply that could come only from a heroic, holy and exactly right personality: '*I'm* in love with Mrs Campbell too, or rather I'd like to be, but something tugs me back.'

Earlyish Work

(TLS, 1978; production at the National Theatre of The Philanderer, *by Bernard Shaw)*

'There is a disease to which plays as well as men become liable with advancing years. In men it is called doting, in plays dating.' So begins the note Shaw prefaced to *The Philanderer* in 1930. I doubt if the play was dating grievously in 1930, when Noël Coward was enjoying a reputation for being highly up-to-the-minute on the strength of just such scenes as the tableau on which *The Philanderer* opens ('A lady and gentleman are making love to one another in the drawing room of a flat in Ashley Gardens . . . It is past ten at night'). And by 1978 Shaw's fear that the play would date in proportion as it had been topical in 1893, the year in which he wrote it but failed to get it put on, has been belied by the whirligig of social history. Women have achieved social emancipation almost as often as the working class, each time with universal amnesia of its ever having happened before. As a result, *The Philanderer* prances onto the too wide stage of the Lyttelton Theatre as the most topical as well as the funniest and the most thoughtful play in town, and the audience easily provides itself with simultaneous mental translation facilities that interpret 'the New Woman' as the Liberated woman.

The Philanderer was Opus 4 of the Celtic School, a school that existed only as a joke between Shaw and Oscar Wilde and lasted only till they discovered their incompatibility. As they contributed plays to it alternately, Opus 4 is Shaw's second play. It comes chronologically, as it does in the text of *Plays Unpleasant*, between *Widowers' Houses* and *Mrs Warren's Profession*. Shaw always seriously aspired to belong to some school or movement — a matter less of socialist conviction than of puritan temperament: he was unable to bear the heady pleasure of creating masterpieces except by persuading himself he was discharging his duty to a cause. Eventually he hitched his aspirations to the most unstoppable movement of all, the evolution of species, of which he could satisfactorily represent both himself as author and his hero John Tanner as helpless tools.

The philanderer himself, Leonard Charteris, is a sketch for Tanner as well as a sketch of Shaw (he looks forward five years to *The Perfect Wagnerite* in his choice of a detached shirt collar 'dyed Wotan blue'), just as the vivisecting doctor contains Shaw's notes for *The Doctor's Dilemma* and the irrefutable case against vivisection he mounted in its Preface. But whereas Tanner, running for his life, tumbles into the net spread for him by Ann Whitefield and the Life Force, Charteris is still a successful evader, though not without cost to his character. He sidesteps so adroitly that he precipitates Julia into an unloving, sentimental marriage to the doctor. A farce can't have had so cruel a neat ending since Rosalind's dismissal of Phoebe, and Shaw's final stage direction admits Julia's 'keen sorrow'.

By the time he created Tanner, Shaw recognised that evolution is all about breeding. Tanner flees domesticity lest it disrupt the intellectual tasks the Life Force sets him. But the Life Force makes him succumb, because it *also* wants him to father the superman. Charteris is still defending his contribution to cultural evolution by dodging any rôle in the biological kind. If the play has a dated patch, it is not where Shaw located it, in the characters' cult of Ibsen. (I suspect, anyway, that Shaw introduced the cult not as a sociological topicality but as an inducement to J. T. Grein, the pioneer Ibsen impresario, to put on the play, plus an advertisement for his own *Quintessence of Ibsenism* of two years before.) Rather, it lies in Shaw's appearance of assuming that the Life Force drives all women, and only women, to nest and breed. Charteris still exists in his thousands, but nowadays half of them are women.

Shaw knew many women who would no more suffer romance or parenthood to interrupt their vocations than he would have done himself. Indeed, the jealousy scene in the first act of *The Philanderer* is based on a 'scene' made in real life by one of Shaw's lovers when she found him with another, the second being the actress Florence Farr, of whom Shaw said that she attached no more importance to love affairs than Casanova or Frank Harris. (In his programme note, Michael Holroyd calls this scene 'unique in that it partly reproduces a dramatic incident that actually took place'. He must have forgotten the wrestling-on-the-sofa scene in *The Applecart*, which had actually taken place between Shaw and Mrs Patrick Campbell.) Had Shaw transcribed into *The Philanderer* the real people as well as the real incident, he would have turned it into *The Philanderer and the Philanderess*.

The reason he didn't was, I suspect, ignorance not of the diversity of women but of contraception. Perhaps he didn't see how a woman *could* have a heterosexual sex life but no babies. His account of his own sex life suggests his ignorance may once have had real-life consequences. 'I was not impotent; I was not sterile; I was not homosexual.' Neither was he a careless user of words. How, as I've murmured elsewhere, did he *know* he was not sterile?

The production at the National Theatre is admirably faithful. The doctor's sitting room does display 'a framed photograph of Rembrandt's School of Anatomy', as Shaw directs it should, though whether the music played on the piano (not by the character Shaw directed) in Act One is truly the beginning of a song called 'When other lips' I am not in a position to tell. The pacing (especially in the second half) and the acting (especially by the two women) are good: good enough, indeed, to make you forget your surroundings and, with them, the fact that one of Shaw's 'causes', the campaign for a national theatre, was posthumously won but also lost when it was realised in a building with the architecture and ambience of a dingy yet pretentious motel.

Major Work

(Souvenir programme, Shaw Festival, Ontario, Canada, 1978)

Shaw paid his first tribute to the devil in 1897. It was, as he pointed out, a product of its century. Dick Dudgeon sides with the devil only because the righteous are hateful. Far from disputing their morality, he swallows it, including the praiseworthiness of self-sacrifice, and puts it into practice — thereby contrasting with the righteous, who only preach it. Even the 'diabolonian ethics' which Shaw draped on Dick in 1900, when he published *The Devil's Disciple* with his other two 'plays for puritans', scarcely fulfil their claim. Shaw traces the literature-long attractiveness of the devil as the victim of a bullying God and he lists the heroic rebels (among the more recent of whom he numbers 'the Overman') who have taken up the devil's cause. But the devil's cause remains as righteous, by God's own standards, as God's.

Between 1901 and 1903, however, Shaw created 20th-century drama and, with it, his religion of social salvation through the evolutionary breeding of a better model of man. He re-translated Nietzsche's *Übermensch* into a more idiomatic (English being a latinate as well as a Germanic language) 'Superman' and incarnated him in one of the folklore rebels against God, Don Juan, who, as dramatised by Mozart and da Ponte, had resisted God's supernatural bullying and gone, terrified but bravely refusing to repent, to hell. Turning the third act of *Man and Superman* into a sequel, set some 50 years on, to Mozart's opera, Shaw brought the devil in person on stage. However, since he had meanwhile evolved the sexy Don Giovanni into a puritan philosopher, the devil, though allowed to be 'clever and plausible', is predestined to the worse of the argument. Shaw must have felt that Dick Dudgeon's ostensible master deserved better at his hands; and in 1905 he finally gave the devil his due and his head in the personage of Andrew Undershaft, 'the hero', as the Preface confesses him to be, of *Major Barbara*.

The City church of St Andrew Undershaft got its name from standing in the shadow of a maypole. English place names often put their emphasis, against sense, on a preposition. (English actors may have learnt their most notorious oral vice from Grange-OVER-Sands and Weston-SUPER-Mare.) When Shaw imagined a foundling in the reign of James I who, after the fashion of the time, supplied his missing proper name from the parish where he was found and who then, in accordance with Shaw's evolutionary doctrine of breeding for brains instead of aristocracy, transmitted his name and his business to a line of selected foundlings, he created a hero whose very name, UNDERshaft, conjures the UNDERworld.

Undershaft's fellow *dramatis personae* are quick to recognise him. To them he is 'Mephistopheles', 'devil', 'demon', 'the Prince of Darkness' and 'a most infernal old rascal', and his place of business is 'this Works Department of Hell'. Shaw (or Corno di Bassetto) clinches the identification by making him proficient on the trombone, the sepulchral instrument whose addition to the orchestra announces (in what Shaw called 'a sound of dreadful joy to all musicians') Don Giovanni's doom.

In *Man and Superman* Shaw 'put', he later said, 'all my intellectual goods in the shop window' — by actually including, in the published version, the text of the revolutionary tract ascribed to his hero. (It contains a presage of 'the Undershaft tradition' in the thought that a stud-farm for breeding Supermen would have to be 'piously disguised as a reformed Foundling Hospital'.) In *Major Barbara* he put all his dramatic goods on the stage. The paradox of a female major has lost piquancy after two world wars in which women wore military uniforms (though even after the second it retained enough to be palely exploited in *Guys and Dolls*), but Shaw makes full use of the Army's picturesqueness and full emotive use of the Salvationists' Authorised-Version language (not least Barbara's 'My God: why has thou forsaken me?', which alarmed the censor of the first production).

His second act is a Dickensian panorama, complete with 'characters' in quite the Dickens manner, of the horrors of unregulated capitalism, his third a prophecy, more frightening than he can have consciously known, of the bland garden suburb of prosperous capitalism, against which some of the prosperous and well-educated young of West Germany and the United States are even now in rebellion, taking to (in Undershaft's, not the Salvation Army's sense) 'Blood and Fire'.

His first act is one of the masterpieces of classical drawing-room comedy. Lady Britomart, whose name (from an obscure Greek divinity, naturalised into English by Edmund Spenser) so trenchantly combines Britannia with a martinet, is, though an estranged, a strongly compatible wife for Undershaft. And indeed Shaw, his evolutionist's eye on heredity, points out that Barbara is her mother's daughter and Sarah her father's, though in both cases against the obvious grain. (It was, however, pointedly in honour of her father's trade that Shaw chose to call Barbara Barbara. St Barbara is the patron saint of gunners.) The Undershaft marriage is the uneasy but effective alliance of capitalism and the Whig aristocracy that governed the British Empire.

Lady Britomart's drawing-room is decorated by an import from that Empire in the form of Adolphus Cusins, a coterie-joke for the first audiences (since he is a portrait of Gilbert Murray, whose version of Euripides occupied the Court Theatre shortly before *Major Barbara*) and also the means whereby Shaw finally transformed the eugenics of aristocracy into the eugenics of evolution, since he turns out to be qualified, on a technicality, to step into the Undershaft inheritance and does so in an episode parallel to the 'recognition scene' of the classical or aristocratic drama wherein the hero regularly qualified for the heroine's hand by proving to be the long-lost son of a duke. By adding intellectual content to both the recognition scene and the character of Lady Britomart, Shaw was perhaps unconsciously re-writing *The Importance of Being Earnest*, which he had reviewed, without praise, ten years before. Indeed, perhaps the otherwise inexplicable blind spot in Shaw's critical vision was induced by the fact that Wilde treated in high farce material that Shaw's imagination already wanted to appropriate for high intellectual comedy.

Over all opponents, and they are all worthy of him, Undershaft triumphs: by demonic force as much as by argument. The Preface makes a rational case for society's collective responsibility for all its acts, including war. On stage, however, Undershaft rejects all offers to whitewash his trade and society's demand for it, refuting the comfortable dogma that the more fearful weapons become, the greater their deterrent value. He knows, in 1905, that technology is stepping up the arms race that will explode in 1914 and that, when he invites Cusins to 'make war on war', he is only making inevitable that 'war to end wars' which, in the event, didn't.

Undershaft has cast off Dick Dudgeon's infatuation with self-sacrifice. He is resolved that, if one man is to grow rich by robbing another into poverty, and if one man is to get his way by dropping bombs on the other, he is not going to be the poor one or the dead one. The 'diabolonian ethics' announced in 1900 became true in 'the Gospel of St Andrew Undershaft'. The final tendency of Shaw's evolutionism, displayed in *Back to Methuselah*, was to rationalise away the destructive instinct in man and the 'problem of evil' in the universe, replacing them with a Life Force which, being blind, makes mistakes. That Shaw allowed a Death Force to speak through Andrew Undershaft is probably part of the debt he acknowledged to Gilbert Murray. Sub-Swinburnian and totally non-Euripidean as Murray's *Bacchae* is, it must have contained enough Euripides, and enough of Euripides's queasy acknowledgement (and warning) of man's unconscious destructiveness, to provoke a flicker of hell-fire from Shaw. Undershaft will keep 'the true faith of an armourer', which is to sell to anyone who can pay a fair price, but he can and will do nothing to ensure that the right side has more of the fair price with which to purchase more of the bullets. Through Undershaft Shaw allows the beauty and terror that humans experience in destruction to express themselves in snatches. He never gave them expression again except in *Heartbreak House*, which was provoked from him by that war to which Undershaft made so massive a contribution.

Saint Mephisto

(TLS, 1981; exhibition, Images of George Bernard Shaw, National Theatre)

Shaw recorded his wife's complaint 'that all the artists and caricaturists, and even the photographers, aimed at producing the sort of suburban Mephistopheles' they imagined him to be. The 'images' that the National Theatre is exhibiting free of entrance charge but subject to initiative test (since you have to perambulate three ill-signposted and not immediately successive levels of Olivier foyer) are chiefly of the personage whom Max Beerbohm named (in a drawing Shaw gave to his secretary Blanche Patch) Mephisto Bernard.

He was, of course, Shaw's invention: a visual counterpart to G.B.S., 'one of the most successful of my fictions'. Indeed, Shaw invented him *avant la lettre* — in the 'frescoes in watercolour' depicting Gounod's Mephistopheles that he executed in boyhood on his bedroom walls at Dalkey. 'When Nature completed my countenance', Shaw wrote, meaning when vaccination let him down and an attack of smallpox in 1881 forced him to leave off shaving, 'I found myself equipped with the upgrowing moustaches and eyebrows, and the sarcastic nostrils, of the operatic fiend whose airs I had sung as a child'. By another anticipation, the scratchy little drawing of his head with its lid off and steam issuing that Shaw sent in a letter of 1904 to Lady Gregory, to assure her that his new play (*John Bull's Other Island*) was seething in his brain, takes palpable shape among the objects the exhibition has borrowed from Ayot St Lawrence, in the form of a Shaw-featured Toby jug (or non-shaving Shavian mug).

It was only in his taste in or nullity about the visual arts, manifest in the architecture and trappings of Shaw's Corner,

97

that Shaw was truly suburban. Had it been built in his lifetime
our National Theatre would be a neo-Tudor barn. What has in
the event been dumped on us is worse yet. The exhibition
presumably honours the fighter for the idea of a national
theatre as well as the author of *Man and Superman*, which is in
repertory, complete with the Mephistophelean third act, in the
Olivier auditorium. But its good will, cramped in any case by
haste (the exhibits are not catalogued, and two at least of the
typewritten captions are in the wrong place), is all but blotted
out by the building's ineptitude. The mean ceilings at headache
height forbid perspectives, deaden the resonance and drama
even of Shaw's ninetieth-birthday talk from the lawn of
Shaw's Corner (which, in the BBC recording of the television
soundtrack, is relayed to the lowest circle of the exhibition),
and drain taboo power from his personal belongings.

Those include, beside bicycles and his typewriter, examples
of his printed postcards, a sample of his Pitman's shorthand
(neat, correct and legible), his raincoat (bearing three
presumably war-time patches) and a tweed cloak in a check of
string colour and (though with his blue/green colour blindness
he couldn't have told) green. His brogues are leather. Plastic
shoes were not yet on sale. He was attacked for the incon-
sistency between his footwear and his vegetarianism —
usually by carnivores too desperate to be acquitted of their
blood guilt to heed his sensible economist's reply that the heart
of the evil was the meat industry, of which leather was a
spin-off.

The shoes also show that he had rather small feet for a rather
tall man — which he was ('Galsworthy and I, as six-footers,
were the most imposing figures', goes his account of pall-
bearing at Hardy's funeral) despite an article in the Spring
newsletter of the National Trust whose author, Robert
Lassam, claims to have met 'a little man' who proved to be
Shaw.

Shaw's smart two-piece bathing suit is on exhibition, and so
is a photograph of him in the act of diving, wearing it. Its two
pieces are designed not to reveal but to overlap and conceal.
Indeed, the only photographs where he is less than at ease are
the ones where he is naked apart from a mistiness of focus and
bathing towel, and takes a stiltedly modest posture. Every-

where else it is he who imposes his Mephistophelean poses on the picture frame.

It is apt that the exhibits are for the most part photographs (including photographs of drawings and paintings), though few will be unknown to possessors of F. E. Loewenstein's *Bernard Shaw Through the Camera* (1948). Shaw made his name by literary journalism, in the exercise of which he restored to English prose a vitality it had lacked since Dryden and Swift. His fame, however, which was belated though colossal, coincided with the rush to success of illustrated mass journalism. The feuilletonist of the 1890s could write: 'You, friendly reader, though you buy my articles, have no idea of what I look like in the street.' By the 1930s you could, and someone did, post an envelope addressed to a sketch of the standard Mephistopheles icon, and get it delivered.

The readers or, strictly, scanners of the popular papers can scarcely have guessed that Shaw was a writer, let alone a great one. In his birthday broadcast he quotes the remark about him that he had not an enemy in the world and none of his friends liked him, attributing it simply to 'one man — a very famous man in his way'. He must have doubted whether the television audience of 1946 would know who Oscar Wilde was. Shaw was following in Wilde's footsteps, though he enlarged and internationalized them, when he became a 'celebrity' celebrated chiefly for his celebrity. He intended the dazzling packet to draw attention to the pills, but the public was quite satisfied just to eat the packet. Shaw was so good at providing it. He trained himself to supply press photographers with bold and interesting subjects as rigorously as he trained himself into a platform orator with pure, sung, Irish vowels and carefully separated and exploded consonants.

Only one photograph makes a personal confession, and it is one where Shaw not only dictated and constituted the subject but, according to the National Trust article, which is about his amateur photography, took the picture himself with a self-timer. He stands at the wayside on crutches, pulling his forelock and holding out his cap to beg. It was in a significant metaphor that he later speculated whether poverty 'lames' people. The crutches in the picture are those on which he limped to his wedding. He did his best to believe that he had waited until he earned 'enough to marry without seeming to marry for money', but he was for ever haunted by the suspicion that it was for financial security that he married his 'Irish millionairess'.

In his scruples and self-accusation he was a typical saint, as well as in his sweetness of temper, the patience of his teaching, his diffidence, his asceticism and the unremitting hard work with which he did what the Life Force bade him. His public mask had to be Mephistopheles. He hoped that, like the villains he impersonated in childhood and unlike the saintly truth, the mask would not 'provoke the antagonism of his hearers'. His wit and his comedic sense, however, are not common among saints, nor yet is his total inability to be cruel or the fact that what the Life Force drove him to was the creation of great literature. In the ninetieth-birthday talk, he suddenly says that being a writer caused him suffering. Aeroplanes whine above the July lawn. It is a final postscript to *Heartbreak House*.

CAA

(She, *1983*)

Every year thousands of our fellow inhabitants of Britain are tricked, tortured, mutilated and killed. None of the main political parties opposes this. One major party explicity supports the practice and promises that, should it win the next general election, it will subsidise the torturers from public funds. The fellow beings of ours at whom this conspiracy is aimed are fish.

Fish have a peculiar effect on humans. That is through no fault of the fish. The fish in our rivers, reservoirs and so forth constitute no danger to us. There is not a single recorded instance where a human, walking by the side of a canal, has been subjected to unprovoked aggression by a fish leaping out of the water and attacking him or trying to drag him in and drown him.

It is we who are the unprovoked aggressors. Walk a mile along a canal bank in Britain and you will see dozens of humans lurking, one by one, in elaborate, expensive and stealthy ambush, dangling in front of the fish what purports to be a free meal but is really the most painful of entrapments, a hook through the lip.

None of these people would offer a child or a dog a bar of chocolate that in fact concealed a hook to be used, after a passage of drawn-out torture that is called, ironically, 'playing' him, to yank him to his death.

It is as though the fact that the fish are there in the water, for most of the time invisible to us, pursuing their own concerns, is something we insist on treating as an insult to us. Dozens of adult humans seem to feel challenged to prove that they are more cunning and more advanced in technology than a fish.

101

Well, of course they are. No contest. Intellectually, it is the humans who are pathetic. But it is the fish who suffers and who is deprived of his life.

The peculiar effect that fish have on humans is to make them forget their humanity and much that goes with it: not only compassion but reason and knowledge.

Consider the sort of conversation I regularly have when a new acquaintance telephones with an invitation to dinner. In common courtesy, before I accept such an invitation I tell our prospective host or hostess that my husband and I are vegetarians. Close friends, of course, already know, and, as it happens, most of them, including our grown-up daughter, are vegetarians too. Indeed, now that vegetarianism is increasing so rapidly, it often turns out that the new host or hostess replies 'So are we' and no further dialogue is needed.

Otherwise, what then takes place goes like this.

'No problem', says host/hostess. 'We love cooking vegetables' or 'I'm particularly proud of my pasta'. That is often followed by 'As a matter of fact, I've often thought I'd like to be a vegetarian myself'.

This was a fashionable thing to say even before April of this year, when Paul McCartney extracted from the Duke of Edinburgh the news that it would not take much persuading to make Prince Charles a vegetarian. As a piece of conversation, however, I find it baffling. There is no shortage of vegetarian food in Britain. To be a vegetarian is the easiest thing in the world, as well as a pleasant one. It is certainly as healthy as being a carnivore and probably healthier, and, though I don't expect this will weigh with the Prince of Wales, it is much, much cheaper. If host/hostess wants to go vegetarian, what, I wonder, is stopping him/her?

Without explaining this point, host/hostess usually continues 'We'll see you on Friday, then. I look forward to cooking a vegetarian meal.' My hand moves to put down the receiver but is interrupted by 'Oh, by the way. You do eat fish, don't you?'

How, I wonder, have so many sane, knowledgeable, well-educated human beings managed to persuade themselves that a fish is a vegetable?

Or consider the Labour Party. I am a member of the Labour

Party and I should naturally like to urge anyone I can to vote for it and, for preference, join it. In general I can urge this without violence to my conscience as a respecter of the rights of animals. For people who recognise that the love of liberty and fairness is claptrap unless you apply it to animals of every species and not just to animals of the human species in whom it is easy to see ourselves reflected, Labour policies stop short of the ideal. Even so, they are the best offered by a major party, and at least they identify the areas where reform is most urgently needed.

They promise priority to discovering and developing methods of scientific research that do not use (or, rather, abuse) animals, to stopping at least the most violent atrocities of 'intensive' farming (farming, that is, in concentration camps) and to introducing laws to ban all hunting with dogs.

In this last item you can hardly say that Labour has gone boldly out on an extremist limb. Opinion polls have been shewing for the last ten years that 60 to 70 per cent of the population would welcome a law banning hunting. Still, the policy as a whole will provoke some flak, chiefly from those who make money from exploiting animals, and it is fair to say that Labour has bravely put reason and decency before electoral caution.

Turn, however, to another section of Labour's campaign document, 'The New Hope for Britain', and you run straight into the Fish Effect — the peculiar response of humans to fish. Labour, we are assured, 'will also provide for wider use of the countryside for recreational purposes, such as angling'. What has destruction to do with any form of creation, including recreation, and why do politicians suppose that people can't enjoy the countryside without causing death?

True, some anglers may be potential Labour voters. But then, so may some thugs who beat up old-age pensioners for fun. Is a political party not to say that beating up old-age pensioners is cruel for fear of losing the thug vote? Does any party want to be known as the self-contradictory party (spare foxes but condemn fish to death)? It is hypocritical to talk about the importance of education if you are scared to inform the citizens that fish are not vegetables or clockwork toys but sentient animals like you and me.

103

Fish are vertebrates like ourselves, though they extract oxygen from the water through gills whereas we extract it from the air through lungs. To be exposed to the air is distressing and ultimately fatal to them in the same way that having our heads forced under water is to us. They function, just as we do, through a brain and a nervous system. There is exactly as much reason to believe that fish feel distress and pain as there is to believe that dogs do or that your next-door neighbour does.

This point was made clearly by a panel that, after sitting for three years under the chairmanship of a zoologist, reported in 1980. The report condemned the cruelty of angling of both kinds.

One kind of angling impales the fish on a hook with the intention that he shall, after torture, die. (And he may not be the only animal to do so. Lines and weights are often left lying about that countryside that Labour wants us to enjoy, where they maim or poison mammals and birds.) The other kind, practised in 'coarse fishing' competitions, impales the fish, hooks him out of his habitat, and imprisons him, often in polluted water, until he has been handled, weighed and measured to boost the angler's competitive ego, after which he is returned to the water he was taken from — very often to die of shock or, slowly, from injuries or infections caused by handling him.

Happily for the good name of the human species, a group was formed in the 1980s called the Campaign for the Abolition of Angling (whose address is P.O. Box 14, Romsey, SO5 9NN). As a new group, it is still small, but my hope is that enough people will join it (which costs very little) to exert an influence on all the parties, and that enough CAA members will then join the Labour Party to persuade it to change its ignorant and illogical mind about fish.

I once met an MP (of a different party) who believed he was a great friend to animals. He opposed all blood sports — except angling. He seriously assured me that fish have no feelings 'because they are cold-blooded'.

I do not think we can afford (and I know the fish cannot afford) legislators whose grasp on elementary biology is so sketchy that they suppose sensation to be transmitted by the

temperature of the blood rather than by the nerve endings —
with which, the Cranbrook Report establishes, the lips and
mouths of fish are 'well endowed'.

In scientific fact, it is a sensitive animal whose lip anglers
pierce and whom they terrorise and do to death under the
pretence of pursuing an innocent and laudable pastime, taking
part in sport and enjoying the countryside.

The name 'coarse' is given to fish whose corpses do not make
delicate eating for humans. But which is truly coarse: the fish
or the bully who considers 'coarse fishing' a sport? And which
is, in the most telling sense, 'cold-blooded': the fish or the
human who tortures him?

Mozart and Jane Austen

(*Spectator*, 1980; The Innocent Diversion, *by Patrick Piggott, Douglas Cleverdon*)

Patrick Piggott yearns for an operatic *Pride and Prejudice* 'with a libretto by, perhaps, Hofmannsthal, and music, of course, by Mozart'. If you acqiesce in that 'of course', you will, I think, be charmed by his book.

The Don Juan whom Jane Austen 'left in hell at half-past eleven' in 1813 was Shadwell's, not Mozart's. The links Mr Piggott traces between her and Mozart are sparse and amusingly shaky. A concert she went to in Bath in 1805 included a Mozart 'overture', which he translates from the idiom of the day into, probably, a symphony. She knew 'Non più andrai' (whose accent he neglects), but under the name 'the Duke of York's New March', thanks to its incorporation by Attwood into an opera of his own. She knew, this time with Mozart's name attached, some variations on an air from *The Magic Flute*.

Besides identifying performances and performers she heard Mr Piggott surveys, in slightly too little detail (it would be nice to know *which* air from the *Flute*), the two surviving Austen family collections of (mainly) keyboard music, some printed, including a Clementi sonata bearing the composer's signature, some privately copied by hands including Jane Austen's, which he finds, and one of his illustrations confirms, to be skilled and elegant.

He doesn't say if there is a copy of 'Malbrook', which the heroine of Lesley Castle pronounces 'the only tune I ever really liked'; but in one of Cassandra Austen's bound-up volumes of the sheet music that originally, he conjectures, belonged to her sister he has found Daniel Steibelt's *Grand Concerto*, a work with an adagio based on 'Annie Laurie' and a once famously noisy 'storm rondo'. He convincingly guesses that the Steibelt is the 'very magnificent' and conveniently loud concerto which Marianne Dashwood plays while Elinor holds her secret and edgy conversation with Lucy Steele. Jane Austen pencilled in some of the fingering on her copy. Mr Piggott concludes that, if she could so much as try to play the work, she was proficient beyond the call of the constant rural-middle-class demand for someone to play music for dancing.

Still, she was less accomplished than her creature Marianne, who, on her first visit to the Middletons', sits down before *their* family collection and sight-reads accompaniment, vocal line and words simultaneously — quite a feat, Mr Piggott points out, for a 17-year-old. The soul of his book is his musical tour of Jane Austen's fictions, which he conducts with uncommon sensibility, worrying about the future of the most ill-used Bennet girl, Mary, and suspecting a 'Freudian slip' when Anne Elliot 'unintentionally' moves towards the piano-forte and the man she loves. (He might have found confirmation in the more explicit incident where Colonel Brandon, for the same cause, moves towards the weeping Marianne 'without knowing what he did'.) He is a guide who takes you into the temple by an unfamiliar route and startles you into noticing, for instance, that the rivalry between Emma Woodhouse and Jane Fairfax is expressed largely as *musical* rivalry, which puts another layer of significance on the mystery of Jane's pianoforte.

So saturated is he in Jane Austen that he feels obliged to warn readers that he often quotes her turns of phrase without quotation marks; and indeed the bulk of his book (or, as he would Austenishly have it, the chief of his book) is couched in a comely quasi-pastiche. Only twice does his archaising play him false. He writes of Jane Austen throughout as an 'authoress' — as she did, of course, of herself: but the word has since changed tone, and I doubt if she would do so now. And he reports Emma's finding Jane Fairfax's reserved replies 'repulsive' without explaining that she uses the word literally (where we might now use the alternative form 'repellent', as in 'water-repellent') to signify that Jane is deliberately repelling Emma's curiosity.

107

There remains the grand paradox. Jane Austen, most operatic of all designers of novels, is only once recorded to have gone to an opera (Arne's *Ataxerxes*), and she found it 'tiresome'. A pianist who practised daily herself, she looked forward to an open-air concert because 'the gardens are large enough for me to get pretty well beyond reach of its sound' and discerned in Miss Holder of Bath the virtue that she 'owns that she has no taste for Music'. Mr Piggott is both practitioner and idolator of music, who evidently takes it for axiomatic that Pater was right about all art aspiring towards the condition of music. The dénouement of *Persuasion*, he claims, 'can only be likened to some of music's finest achievements', and, in particular, to the final act of the *Flute*. (In reality there seems no sound reason why it should not be likened to some of architecture's or painting's or even to some other of literature's own finest achievements.) His feelings are hurt by Jane Austen's anti-music remarks, as they are by the triviality of some of the music she owned. He doesn't, however, wriggle like pious Browning trying to shew that *his* idol, Shelley, couldn't have *really* been an atheist, but admits she was sometimes 'disconcertingly philistine' and humbly suggests that the mechanicalness of piano practice gave her an opportunity to plan her books.

He might, I think, have conjectured further. Like many artists in prose, she probably envied the direct emotional expressiveness of music. (This isn't idolatrous. Composers may equally envy the concrete content of literature, and Mozart declared that his 'greatest desire' was 'to write operas'.) Indeed, I imagine that the clue to her ambivalence lies in the expressiveness — or the provocativeness — of music, including trivial music ('Extraordinary how potent cheap music is'). Elinor Dashwood is 'neither musical, nor affecting to be so'; Marianne *is* musical, without affectation, certainly, but with an impractical, self-destructive will to encourage her own emotions to express themselves at highest pitch through music. Jane Austen chose to lead a disciplined life not only as amateur pianist but as creator and person. It may be that she was sometimes philistine about music because she sometimes found music too moving to bear.

Mozart and da Ponte

(1981, programme book for Royal Opera House, Covent Garden; Musical Times)

'I like an aria to fit a singer', Mozart remarked by letter to his father, 'as perfectly as a well-made suit of clothes.' Lorenzo da Ponte fitted his librettos to their composers with the same bespoke accuracy. He was the first (and last) of Mozart's librettists, and perhaps among the first of his admirers, to study and understand the nature of Mozart's operatic genius. As sheer genius, it stunned him. Mozart, he judged in the memoirs he wrote at 60, was perhaps superior to 'any other composer in the world, past, present or future'. But he also recognized it, analytically and practically, as a genius that 'demanded a subject which should be ample, elevated and abounding in character and incident'.

The subject Mozart proposed to him, which became in 1786 the subject of their first collaboration, was *Le mariage de Figaro*. It was the sole large-scale occasion when Mozart united his music to a positive literary masterpiece. Da Ponte was inspired by Beaumarchais's genius as well as Mozart's. He turned a French five-act play with 16 rôles into an Italian four-act libretto with eleven, two of which, he noted, could be doubled (and, at the first production, were), and yet did no violence to Beaumarchais's classic structure.

With equal skill, he kept the revolutionary core of the play intact. The spoken play was forbidden, by Joseph II personally, in the Vienna theatre. Da Ponte secured permission for the opera by explaining to the emperor that, in order to make space for the music, he would have to cut the text extensively, which would cut out its political offensiveness. The explanation was specious. Da Ponte cut Beaumarchais's lines but expanded his images. The 'et puis dansez, Monseigneur' of Beaumarchais's Figaro is translated into the most militant of arias, an explicit warning that encroachments by the ruling class will be resisted by the workers, 'Se vuol ballare, signor Contino'. The relationships in the play are expanded into the sustained ensembles in which Mozart can display both sides of a confrontation in action simultaneously, thus making it dramatically clear that the Count's arbitrary and self-interested exercise of aristocratic authority is met by a popular alliance of three oppressed classes, namely servants, women and the young.

It was in May 1783 that Mozart reported from Vienna to his father in Salzburg that 'our poet here is now a certain Abbate da Ponte' and went on to exclaim 'I should dearly love to shew what I can do in an Italian opera!' (What he could do in a German opera he had shewn the year before, in *Die Ent-führung*.) Da Ponte, drawn to Vienna by the news that Joseph II intended to re-establish Italian opera there, arrived knowing neither German nor any Germans. Part of his stock-in-trade was, indeed, being a native Italian speaker. The facts that the earliest operas and the first operatic masterpieces were Italian were matters of, respectively, musical history and the personal genius of Monteverdi. But the persistence of Italian opera a couple of centuries later, side by side with opera in the native language, at the capitals and courts of German-speaking states was a matter, at least in part, of political history and, in particular, of the large Austrian territorial possessions in Italy. Moreover, Austria maintained the political fiction that its European land empire was a Holy (that is, Catholicized) version of the ancient Roman empire, in token of which the emperor bore, among others, the title of Caesar Augustus, and the court poet (that is, librettist) the title *Poeta Cesareo*, 'Caesarean Poet'. Imperialism opened the route to Vienna for Italian opera, much as imperialism opened the route to Britain for Indian restaurants; and at the same time the Italianness of opera at Vienna reinforced the empire's claim to be Roman and, if not holy, at least cosmopolitan and cultivated.

The Italian opera drew Italian-born composers like Salieri and Paisiello to Vienna, set a premium on Italian singers (da

Ponte complained that the choruses of his first libretto for Salieri were destined to be sung by Germans) and offered large opportunities (but also large rivalries) to literary Italians, like da Ponte, capable of writing interestingly in Italian that was idiomatic yet not abstruse; for, as Mozart had discovered in 1780, when he was composing *Idomeneo* in Munich and asking for changes in the text to meet his own and the singers' requirements, 'far-fetched or unusual words are always unsuitable in an aria that ought to be pleasing'.

Da Ponte's native ground was in the Venetian Republic. Under the patronage of the local bishop, whose name he took, he got himself an education in a seminary, judged, correctly, that he had no vocation for the priesthood and became a teacher in another seminary, where, however, he wrote a rhetorical exercise on Rousseauist lines which resulted in his being banned from teaching in the Republic. He picked up a living by literary sponging, gambling and draughts playing, meanwhile discovering a private vocation for complex love affairs and feuds, until, in his early 30s, he took the route opened by imperialism towards his professional vocation. He arrived at Dresden, where the court poet was Caterino Mazzolà, whom da Ponte so frightened by his patent ambition to replace him that Mazzolà sent him on to Vienna bearing a letter of recommendation to Salieri.

His first libretto was indeed for Salieri, and Mozart was initially afraid that da Ponte was too committed to Salieri to write for *him*. He therefore sent home the suggestion that Varesco, the librettist of *Idomeneo*, should write him a new libretto, for which he provided an exact specification: a 'really comic' story and seven characters, including 'two equally good female parts, one of these to be *seria*, the other *mezzo carattere* . . . The third female character, however, may be entirely *buffa*, and so may all the male ones'. Ultimately, it was da Ponte who (almost exactly) filled Mozart's prescription.

At Vienna, da Ponte singled out only two composers as worthy of his respect, though he considered them 'almost complete opposites' in style: Martin y Soler, a Spaniard who held the imperial favour, and Mozart, who da Ponte thought could win it. He complained afterwards that Mozart's early biographers cheated him of his credit for promoting Mozart's operatic career.

Da Ponte had glimpsed his vocation in childhood, when he read and re-read Metastasio. At Vienna he met the aged Metastasio, and when Metastasio died, after holding the post of 'Caesarean Poet' for the greaster part of the 18th century, he formed the ambition to succeed him. So, however, did another Italian librettist, Giovanni Battista Casti, who had the ear of the theatre management. The imperial theatre was doubly prone to intrigue, being both a theatre and a bureaucracy. Da Ponte's own propensity for intrigue perhaps contributed to his mastery of imbroglio in plots, but in real life he was a blunderer with a chip on his shoulder and, often, a victim. A blunder finally cost him his place at Vienna. He moved on to London and, eventually and sadly, to New York; and Mozart's last Italian opera was, ironically, to a text by Metastasio, adapted into a 'real opera', as Mozart noted, by Mazzolà.

Da Ponte might have been designed by destiny to write for Mozart. They shared liveliness of temperament. Da Ponte characterized his own childhood by words that apply to Mozart's: 'liveliness of speech', 'readiness of reply', 'insatiable curiosity'. They turned the same commonsense vision on theatrical detail, da Ponte objecting to being required to bring all the characters on stage for a finale in defiance of reason as well as Aristotle, Mozart excising an aside from an aria in *Idomeneo* on the grounds that, implausible enough in itself, it would be doubly so when repeated. Both resented the sycophancy imposed by princely patronage. Both rebelled against a social system where artists worked without end and barely scraped a living. Da Ponte was, like Mozart, bold in artistic judgments, complaining of 'the difficulties of writing verses for a composer who was a fool' (Peticchio) and recording that 'the bad opinion I had of the composer' (Righini) 'stifled my inspiration'. Most Italian librettos he found dross, an opinion Mozart shared when, still despairing of securing da Ponte as his librettist, he 'looked through at least a hundred' and found hardly one to his taste. Da Ponte learnt his craft not from precedents but from practice, the precedents having taught him that 'it was not enough to be a great poet . . . in order to write a good play'.

At the end of the year in which the Anglo-Italian Nancy

Storace 'created' the role of Mozart's and da Ponte's Susanna, da Ponte provided her brother Stephen with the libretto for his rather Figaresque *Gli equivoci* (which had a production in London in 1974), in which the pruning knife he had sharpened on Beaumarchais was most effectively applied to the repetitious mistaken identities of *The Comedy of Errors*. For Martin in the same year he adapted a Spanish play into *Una cosa rara*. Da Ponte at first kept his name off the libretto in order to have the laugh on his enemies when the opera succeeded. (Mozart was citing two of the peaks of his librettist's career when he quoted from *Una cosa rara* as well as *Figaro* among the current hit tunes played at Don Giovanni's supper.) In the next year he wrote for Martin *L'arbore di Diana* (which had a revival in London in 1972), an invented (by da Ponte) addition to mythology whereby Cupid, with the help of a magic apple tree, overcomes Diana's inveterate taste for chastity. Martin's music is charming, and da Ponte thought the text his best work, 'full of love and yet not lascivious'.

Da Ponte wrote *Diana* contemporaneously with two other librettos. With a bottle of Tokay to the right of his table (clearly he had been quick to take up the sweets of the Austro-Hungarian union), an inkstand in the middle and a tobacco box to the left, sustained by the housekeeper's daughter on coffee and flirtation, he worked 12 hours a day, writing for Martin in the morning, in the evening for Salieri, for whom he was Italianizing an opera Salieri had already composed in French, and at night for Mozart. He had suggested Don Giovanni as the subject for the opera Mozart had been commissioned to provide for Prague.

Da Ponte probably intended Don Juan, libertine and free-thinker, to be another socially rebellious hero like Figaro. Mozart, da Ponte said later, gave the opera a serious turn from the outset. In picking the subject, da Ponte had bound himself to a plot that had to be developed as a linear succession of incidents. It had swiftness, which suited both da Ponte and Mozart, but it lacked the structural balances and ironies that da Ponte was good at. He was, besides, much less at ease with this vengeful bit of Christian folklore than with classical paramythology. Perhaps some inherent uncertainty in da Ponte's tone became the vehicle for Mozart's own violently ambivalent

113

emotions, guilty yet defiant, after his father's death. Da Ponte's competent rendering of fustian melodrama is carried by Mozart to unsurpassed extremes of spiritual melocrama. Don Giovanni is villain and yet hero brave enough to refuse to repent even though supernaturally bullied by the chill of the tomb itself.

Don Giovanni was given (but not much liked) at Vienna and *Figaro* successfully revived there before da Ponte and Mozart produced, in January 1790, their final work together, the opera that fulfilled (except that there are, symmetrically, six characters, not seven) Mozart's recipe of seven years earlier. The sisters in *Così* are indeed 'two equally good female parts', one of them *seria*. The third woman is indeed *buffa* − the maidservant whom da Ponte, wisps of seminary learning still about him, named by the Italianized ancient Greek word for 'the mistress of the house'. Da Ponte perhaps drew on his own experience of being equally in love with two sisters in Dresden, Mozart perhaps on his of falling in love with one Weber sister and then falling in love with and marrying another. The story is indeed 'really comic' − and much besides: a masterpiece of tragicomic irony, a 'school for lovers' (the subtitle and the name by which da Ponte mentions the opera in his memoirs) whose two pairs of lover-pupils learn painfully that it is not reasonable to expect either one's sweetheart or oneself to be superhuman. The partnership that opened with *Le Nozze di Figaro* shut up shop on the unillusioned marriages of Fiordiligi and Dorabella and is itself one of the world's perfect marriages between literary and musical drama.

Mozart the Letter-Writer

(LRB, 1986; The Letters of Mozart and his Family, *translated and edited by Emily Anderson, third edition, Macmillan)*

Mozart the letter-writer, like Mozart the composer of virtually every form and species of music, is the supreme non-bore. The 'daughter of Hamm, the Secretary for War,' must, he reports to his father from Augsburg in 1777, have a gift for music since, even without having been well taught, she can play several clavier pieces 'really well'. Yet she is an affected performer. Tuition in Salzburg from Mozart *père* would improve both her musical knowledge and her intelligence, and the teacher would get 'plenty of entertainment' in return. 'She would not eat much, for she is far too simple. You say that I ought to have tested her playing. Why, I simply could not do so for laughing. For whenever, by way of example, I played a passage with my right hand she at once exclaimed Bravissimo! in a tiny mouse-like voice.'

It is easy to imagine how Mozart would have set the word for such a voice.

He goes on to recount an enthusiastic proposal to arrange a concert for him in Augsburg and then the proposer's wriggling out, when he 'remarked quite coolly: "Look here, a concert is quite out of the question. Oh, I assure you, I lost my temper yesterday on your account. The patricians told me that their funds were very low and that you were not the type of virtuoso to whom they could offer a souvrain d'or." I smiled and said "I quite agree"'. At luncheon there is no mention of the concert. 'After lunch I played two concertos, improvised something and then played the violin in one of Hafeneder's trios. I would gladly have done some more fiddling, but I was accompanied so badly that it gave me the colic.' His well-to-do hosts take him to the theatre. Returned, he plays again before supper, where, between offerings of snuff, which he reciprocates, he is teased about his cross. By shome neo-editorial mishtake, which Mozart would have delighted to pounce on, the footnote numbers have been jiggled in the turning of a page and the cross seems to be glozed in the new edition as a 'local term for the large hall in the Augsburg Rathaus', in fact the site of the proposed concert. Application to the previous edition makes it clear that Mozart was wearing the Order of the Golden Spur, given him seven years before by Pope Clement XIV. The supper party speculates that the cross is not gold but copper. 'Burning with anger', Mozart declares it to be tin. Perhaps thanks to his threat to quit Augsburg at once, Mozart received and reported in the next few days a quasi-apology, some courtesy from some powerful citizens, a further suggestion for a concert (which he eventually gave) and, after further playing of music, two ducats, delivered much in the manner of a modern tip but without the supposed tax advantage.

The invaluable gift of mounting vivid detail on a coherent strategic skeleton makes Mozart an incomparable creator of operas. 'You know my greatest desire is — to write operas', he tells his father in 1778. 'Do not forget', he adds in a later passage in the same letter, 'how much I desire to write operas'. The gift of vividness was transmitted to him by Leopold Mozart, perhaps partly through heredity but also and visibly by expectation and example, as part of Mozart's musical, social and general aesthetic training. The translated text begins with Leopold Mozart's letter to his landlord and banker: 'You have been thinking, haven't you, that we are already in Vienna? But we are still in Linz.' He is precisely imagining his correspondent's thoughts in the manner that it was vital for Mozart, as composer and performer, to imagine with precision his audience's response.

The letters exchanged by the Mozart family have the purpose of many 18th-century letters: to sustain intimacy and to create the intimacy of shared experience even through separations.

Emily Anderson's masterly rendering into English of the Mozarts' German and, when it occurs at length, Italian was

116

first issued in 1938 in three volumes. In 1966, by which time Emily Anderson was dead, a second edition gave evidence of the simultaneous waxing and waning that is the work's publishing history. Revised and augmented, it became the most complete version available in any language of all Mozart's surviving letters and of those by his immediate family written to or largely about him. Yet although it had grown it shrank from three volumes to two.

The new (third) edition shrinks further: to a single volume. The paper has lost weight and the page size is diminished. Yet the pages begin and end on the same words of the text as in the previous edition. Revision seems confined to the prefatory editorial pages and the indices that follow the text, the footnotes at the ends of the pages and the margins of the pages.

Into those margins the new version of the work introduces asterisks and square brackets. According to the publisher's preface, they respectively indicate, though they do not correct, omissions and 'substantially paraphrased passages' in the text alongside. As the eccentric result, the text flows down some pages between banks that look littered with fragments of barbed wire.

The prefatory editorial matter has increased from 35 pages in the two-volume edition to 46 in the new single volume. The illustrations occur no longer one-by-one but in clumps. They have lost the numbers they bore in the list in the previous edition. A footnote in the new edition, however, still bids you 'See illustration no. 10'. That is now a nonsense instruction.

An editorial amendment that would have been helpful is not made. When the text opens, the Mozart children, accompanied by both parents, are making the second of their journeys. So much the editorial explanation that precedes each chunk of letters makes clear both in the previous and in the new version. The new version might have usefully added that Nannerl Mozart was eleven and Wolfgang (whom his father writes of as 'Woferl') six, rather than leave the reader to find out from other sources.

Indeed, it would have been useful and easy to insert a brief preliminary table of the dates of birth, marriage and death of the main Mozarts. It should have replaced the table of monetary values, said anyway to be 'only approximate'. The tip Mozart was given in Augsburg is not much clarified by the information that the ducat was in 1938 worth about nine shillings or (as the new volume adds in brackets) in 1985 about thirteen and a half United-States dollars. Size would have been more to the point than value given that Mozart was at six beset by sores, presently diagnosed as Viennese scarlet-fever spots and ascribed to the change of air. As though tragically prescient of his son's lifelong lack of money and health, Leopold Mozart called them 'as large as a kreuzer'.

Editorially, the new volume is a bit of a botch, seemingly more anxious to put down markers, civil-service fashion, than to help readers. It should help the editors of a future edition. With this one you have, as with Mozart's own untidy manuscripts, to read through the ink splutters.

The reward is a powerful glimpse of Mozart's greatness and Emily Anderson's careful and sensitive work.

Attempting, perhaps, a pre-emptive strike on criticism, the publisher's preface to the new volume remarks that it 'has from time to time been pointed out' that Miss Anderson, as it calls her, 'does not always reflect the quicksilver changes of mood and of tempo in Mozart's own literary style and provides it with a fluent literacy that is wanting in the original'. Sensible readers will remember how many 18th-century letters, in whatever language, by deeply literate people are wayward in orthography and punctuation. The publisher has had the sense to reprint but not, it appears, to read Emily Anderson's own introduction to her translation. After speaking of the hurry, spontaneity and slang of Mozart's letter-writing style, for which she has sought equivalents while avoiding transient fashions, she remarks that his 'liveliness and haste are reflected too in his punctuation. Very often whole letters are a series of sentences strung together by dashes. As a slavish adherence in this respect to the originals would have produced pages wearisome to the eye of the reader, the letters have been punctuated more normally and the dashes retained only where the sense demands it.'

The dust-up in Augsburg, which figured to him as paternal territory ('"I should never in my life have believed that in Augsburg, my father's native town, his son would have been so insulted"'), was the precursor of those acts by Mozart, notably his break with his ecclesiastical employer in Salzburg, his relation to the Weber family and his marriage to one of it, which Leopold Mozart read as rebellions against himself, God or the social order. They prompted him to circumspect yet sometimes sly cautions. Mozart's rebellions are to be read, I do not doubt, in the nonsense fantasies about shitting and pissing that occur in his letters (and, as Emily Anderson, who translated the passages unexpurgated, was right to point out, not only his letters to his cousin Maria Anna Theckla Mozart). The psychoanalytic significance of the passages only begins with money, about which so many of Leopold Mozart's cautions and precepts circle. They serve also the social purpose of the letters by reconstituting the intimacy and, which is important, the equality of people who were once small children together — so far as Mozart's precocious and cherubic gift left him time ever to *be* a child. In full and beautiful form his rebellions are to be heard in the response of his imagination to the libretti he selected or accepted as skeletons for operas: the all but open revolutionary import of *Le Nozze di Figaro* and the reactionary, counter-Reformation import of *Don Giovanni*, where the rebel-hero incurs supernatural punishment but bravely and honestly refuses to repent even when bullied by the threat of hell.

The psychological centre of the letters is Mozart's relationship with the father who was also tutor, worldly instructor, religious preceptor, agent and manager. Virtually from the outset Mozart knew, and knew from his father's tutoring, that he was to prove himself a biddable and obedient pupil and to incur both triumph and guilt by excelling his father in their common profession. Mozart transcended the psychologically agonising trap by the creation of great music. His move into transcendence is documented by the inspired and workmanlike letters they exchanged in 1780 during the composition and mounting of *Idomeneo*. Mozart is in Munich, where mutes for trumpets and horns are not to be had. He asks his father to send one of each (for copying) from Salzburg by the mail coach. At the same time he negotiates through his father with the librettist, the ecclesiastic Varesco, who is also in Salzburg. Suggesting that the utterance of the subterranean voice in the libretto for *Idomeneo* would be rendered more effective if it

119

were shortened, Mozart asks his father to perform the imaginative act whose importance he had learned from his father's example. 'Picture to yourself the theatre, and remember that the voice must be terrifying — must penetrate — that the audience must believe that it really exists.' The audience's belief will crumble away, he argues, if the voice goes on too long and he suggests an amendment to another text, also a father-and-son story: 'If the speech of the Ghost in Hamlet were not so long, it would be far more effective.'

Sigmund Freud, the explicator of father-and-son stories, expressed his own sentiments of social rebellion by singing ('possibly another person would not have recognised the tune') Figaro's *Se vuol ballare, signor Contino* to himself as he waited on a railway station in Vienna. Freud, our era's peer to Aristotle in analytic imagination and an informed classicist, agreed with Aristotle's *Poetics* in placing Sophocles's *Oedipus the King* at the centre and summit of Greek tragedy. Yet Greek mythology provides another father-and-son story, and one where it is the father who is trapped between his duty to a god and his duty to and love for his son, though it is the son who is to pay. On his way home from the Trojan War, Idomeneus, king of Crete, escapes drowning, when his ship is wrecked, by vowing to sacrifice the first live being he meets on dry land. He meets his now grown-up (the Trojan War did last) son. In mythology Idomeneus either carries out the sacrifice or tries to do so, and as a result the people depose and exile him.

That ending Mozart's librettist, Varesco, softened in a secondary elaboration (which seems to have been original to him though he was writing an Italian adaptation of a French libretto made into an opera early in the eighteenth century). The operatic Idomeneo abdicates in favour of his son. The concept of an authoritative father who *wills* his own supercession by his son made it possible, I believe, for Mozart both to negotiate through his tutor-manager-father and to create his first transcendent opera. Buyers of recordings and opera audiences in many civilised cities nowadays have the opportunity to know *Idomeneo* as closely as they know *Figaro*. Had turn-of-the-century Vienna yet made that laudable and important enlargement of taste, Freud might have identified and named the Idomeneus Complex.

In Praise of Ms Navratilova

(Spectator, 1981)

Not since the early years of the industrial revolution has there been a lowlier working life. During the service the net cord judge has to crouch with his head on one side, his ear to the wire and his finger on its pulse; the rallies are usually the occasion for him to flinch and strain backwards in his chair for fear of being thumped by a misdirected passing shot. He is a target also for reproach, since players often hear a net cord where he hears none. John McEnroe seemed for an instant in the course of his singles semi-final to be invoking the umpire's compassion for the net cord judge. 'He's a human being,' he protested. But he went on to explain what he meant by that: 'He can make mistakes.'

To my mind the net cord judge ought not to be a human being. He is ripe for automation. Wimbledon has installed electronic monitors to check whether a service lands in the service court. Those, however, have to perform a complex task by a method (registering when a beam is interrupted) not precisely appropriate, since what counts is where the ball touches down, not the airspace it traverses in getting there. The monitors are known to be fallible, are sometimes over-ruled and are as likely to provoke disputes as to cure them. By contrast it would, I surmise, be easy to render the wire inside the top of the net sensitive to impact, and the result would be infallible. (Birds and heavy insects are not given to perching on the net, but if one did he would be seen and discounted.) As for line calls (of all kinds, not just service faults): on the show courts at least, which are covered by BBC television, a more effective check than the electronic monitors is at hand. All you need is a television set beside the umpire's chair. That would

121

make the replay of a disputed point available to umpire and players, and it would settle the question in all but the rare cases when the camera is unsighted.

The only danger in virtually infallible monitoring is that it might deprive Wimbledon of Mr McEnroe's best (which is distinct from his most point-winning) tennis. Bjorn Borg's best, paradoxically signalled when he abandons his natural station on the baseline and takes to volleying, was extracted, in their semi-final, by the invention and unremitting will-to-win of Jimmy Connors. But such is Mr McEnroe's Irish appetite for suffering injustice that he was, in his opening match, beating Tom Gullikson in a rather plodding way until, in the third set, he was the victim of some patently wrong calls. That set off his first famous outburst, the one where he called the umpire 'the pits of the world'. (I liked Nancy Banks-Smith's suggestion that it was a case of life being just a bowl of cherry pits, but the more plausible gloze, whereby 'pits' was short for 'armpits', gave the thing a certain Old Testament exoticism: 'my beloved is the armpits of the world', as it were.) Only after being docked a penalty point did he begin to play the tennis if not of an angel at least of a baroque *putto*, an image rounded off by the childish token of effort, a plump protrusion of tongue from mouth, as he serves.

Tennis is intrinsically frustrating, because it's all headlong courses that may have to be suddenly braked. Its nature is epitomised by the two bites the server has at the service and by the system whereby to win a game or a set you have to be not one but two points or games ahead. That system is the intellectual brilliance of tennis as an invention, and what is brilliant about it is that it constantly gives your opponent a chance to frustrate your strategic planning. The players have now acquired voices to express their frustration. Wimbledon has always been a touch militaristic (witness its passion for putting people into uniform, a passion intensified now that it can no longer enforce pure and graffiti-free white on the players), and it is now shewing the characteristic hurt bafflement of an officer class whom 'the men' have taken to answering back. (If it would just adopt the obvious monitors I've named, authority would no longer be posing as infallible in the first place, and would finish with less mud in its eye.) Umpires still use the formula 'Smithers to serve' but when they address the player directly they now call him 'Mr Smithers', a courtesy wrested from them by the original and still best tantrum-thrower, Ilie Nastase. Their trouble is that they then seem to have nothing to say. The inarticulacy of umpires who, asked to explain their decisions, merely repeat the decision has made Mr McEnroe the hero of the anti-authoritarians. I think they've mistaken their man. He is not a champion of justice. He is an advocate. What he pleads is usually, so far as my eye and the replay can tell, true. But the only cause he pleads is his own. In his semi-final with Rod Frawley he stormed at the umpire: 'All I want to see is just one call in my favour.' Alas, the umpire was precluded (not this time by inarticulacy but by loyalty to his own earlier bad judgment) from pointing out that he had, a minute or two before, confirmed a glaringly wrong call against Mr Frawley.

This seeming need to feel unjustly used by authority is a variation on the problem many players visibly experience in finding the appropriate image of themselves for their imaginations to inhabit in a particular match. Mr Borg, the most effective of counter-attacking players, can drop a first game or even set without harm, because he slips into the strategy and psychology of the fight-back. He was ill at ease in the final from the moment Mr McEnroe insisted on dropping the first set to *him*. Martina Navratilova lost to Hana Mandlikova because she would not surrender her belief that in any confrontation she is the one who plays the unorthodox, dashing (if sometimes slapdash) and piratical (hence the bandana headband) tennis. I think she will be vulnerable to younger exponents of her own romantic and risky style until she gets the knack of delighting in herself as a foxy old master, a self-image that was the secret, I suspect, of Rod Laver's late-developing but long-lasting mastery.

Although some players are known, in a quasi-technical term, as 'artists', tennis is not an art. The players are not striving to create a beautiful match, but to win. There are no marks, as in competitive skating, for 'artistic impression'. Even so, the Muses sometimes nudge the seeding committee. This year they were at fault in ordaining that one of the two most beautiful games in women's tennis, Ms Navratilova's and

Ms Mandlikova's, must be eliminated before the final, and from an aesthetic point of view it was the wrong one that went out. Not only did Dan Maskell demonstrate that Czechoslovakia is still a far-away country of whose nomenclature we know nothing by his apparent refusal to believe that Ms Mandlikova's father, who was watching, could bear a surname not to the letter identical with hers (he spoke of him under what I take to be the hermaphrodite form, 'Mr Mandlikova'); but the beauty of Ms Mandlikova's game, which had flowered over the courts in earlier rounds, was crushed in advance of the final by the weight of the occasion. The Muses did, however, lay on a classically beautiful quarter-final between Mr Connors and Vijay Amritraj. If players were divided, like sopranos, into dramatic and lyric, here was a top instance of each. Mr Amritraj possesses the comeliest style since Mr Nastase was at his peak. He took enough points to set the umpire the persistent tongue-twister 'Advantage — Amritraj' and did it by tennis of such grace as to refashion Wimbledon into one of those pastoral miniatures where Krishna sports with the milkmaids.

In the future this Wimbledon may be noted as the first to see the talents of Corinne Vanier and Kathy Rinaldi. It felt like the first Wimbledon of an approaching ice age. I wonder what sort of playing surface tundra will make? And now it's over I wonder whether John McEnroe *père* will crown his son's championship by divulging to him that useful secret of adult life, how to secure one's shoelaces with a double knot?

Lawn Tennis: feminine or female

(*Listener*, 1977)

The fact that women's tennis is a slightly different game from tennis must, I think, be the result of the peculiar way in which tennis (that is, lawn tennis in general) evolved. Older sports grew up as sports for men and were later moved in on by women. Lawn tennis, however, was invented as a game for the sexes to play communally. Indeed a comprehensive history of how members of the middle class met the people they married would have to include a chapter on the tennis party and the tennis club. Yet, anomalously, from the moment that first-class public competition began, players of different sex have never competed against each other — except in mixed doubles, which is, in consequence, a very different game from all the other varieties. In first-class mixed doubles, the *type* of tennis each partner plays is fore-ordained according to sex, in a division as formal as the sexual division of the dancing rôles in classical ballet.

Tennis is a bisexual game that suddenly, when it reaches first-class standard, splits into sexual compartments. First-class women's tennis has its own history of 'separate development', and what it has developed as is a repertoire of substitutes and compensations. It is as if a whole sect of early players had or believed they had a weak backhand and therefore evolved and passed on to their successors a game in which it was standard practice for everyone to run round his backhand in order to play all strokes forehand.

So far as historical results go, it makes little difference whether the disabilities for which the women's game compensates were physiological or matters of inhibition. Both are entirely 'real' in effect. The sole indisputably physiological disadvantage to a woman player, if you imagine her facing a man at a Wimbledon singles final, is that there is a one in six chance that she would be menstruating that day. Even that handicap is now tameable by The Pill, but it is entirely possible that some potential champion of the past is unknown to history because of a synchronisation between her menstrual cycle and the second week of Wimbledon.

For that disability women's tennis could provide no substitute. All it could do was confine competition to people who at least might be labouring under the same disability. For other supposed disabilities, the women's game developed highly skilled and sophisticated compensations: in place of a forceful service, spin and disguise; in place of net-rushing, a subtle, accurate and exhausting process of manoeuvring from the baseline.

These skills the women's game developed in compensation for disabilities which, as pioneers in each case proved, turned out not to be physiological at all. That is, they were not necessarily present in all women, though they might be in some women (and in some men). It was widely believed that women couldn't volley (or couldn't volley effectively), let alone bound about the court, until Suzanne Lenglen demonstrated otherwise at the legendary Wimbledon of 1919. At Wimbledon 1977, some woman will use each of the tennis tactics which all women were once believed incapable of. And some women will use hardly any of them — either because they, as individuals, can't or because (like, supremely, Chris Evert) they play the traditional women's game to such perfection that they can nearly always overcome nearly all the exponents they meet of flexible (or bisexual) tennis.

Equally, of course, not all the men players will use all the tactics once thought the prerogatives of men. Not every man in first-class tennis wields the vehement service of a Virginia Wade or a Martina Navratilova. Indeed, if women's tennis is, technically, the tennis of using craftiness, timing and anticipation as aggressive substitutes for force, then the finest living players of women's tennis are Ken Rosewall and Rod Laver.

Either of them (or any man player of first-class forceful tennis) could, I don't doubt, wipe the best women players off court. The adage that a top man can beat a top woman

126

remains true. However, Billie Jean King has narrowed its margin of certainty by shewing that a present top woman can beat a past top man, and it very much looks as if history (alike of tennis and of women) is now drawing a deep breath with the intention of blowing the old adage away.

Tennis in general has progressed by shedding inhibitions — frequently along with garments, which no doubt symbolised and must have physically reinforced them. Women had to discard the inhibiting belief that thumping the ball was 'unladylike' (a class inhibition) or 'unfeminine' (a sexual one) as well as being, as it is to thumpers of either sex, a risk of inaccuracy. (I think it was Christine Truman in the early Sixties who burst through that inhibition in first-class women's tennis, though of course it had long been disregarded, at great cost to accuracy, on recreation grounds throughout the country.) Equally, though it managed to do so some decades earlier, the men's game had to discard the notion that it was a touch 'unsporting' to win.

Even the inhibitions imposed by unsuitable clothing were not imposed exclusively on women. True, the tennis clothes of the 1880's did weigh more heavily on women than on men, since the women were swaddled in long skirts and the now scarcely imaginable things worn under them. (Elizabeth Ryan, a persistent winner of Wimbledon doubles titles between 1914 and the mid-Thirties, attributed her success to 'taking off my girdle'.) But the men who played in wide-brimmed hats, which must have threatened to rise from the head whenever the wearer ran, probably undertook an even worse disability than the women, whose hats, though more elaborate, were no doubt skewered on.

Some of the early men players had, of course, the sense to play hatless or in no more than a cricket cap. And perhaps the first time a woman triumphed over female opposition by adopting a tactic from the men's game was in 1887, when Lottie Dod, at the age of 15, won the Wimbledon singles in (to judge from her portrait photograph — the books say she played in her school uniform) a cricket cap.

It was Lenglen who, as well as discarding the inhibition against volleying, reduced the women's hats to a mere token bandeau (since revived by Bjorn Borg). Even she, however,

127

played in stockings, though in the more bounding photo-graphs you can detect that they came to a presumably elasticated top just above the knee. Women didn't regularly play bare-legged until the Thirties. At that time, as if by contrariness, the men players, whose tennis trousers had until then had tolerably narrow legs, went into wide trouser legs that must have been aerodynamic disasters. I imagine that's why, in 1932, H. W. Austen pioneeringly appeared on court in shorts.

When the women's game discarded inhibitions of style, it usually did so by way of imports from the men's game. Indeed, experience of the men's game discernibly gave some of the early women an advantage over female opposition. Rose Payten, a New South Wales champion from 1900 to 1907 and judged the best woman player of the time, is recorded (by Lance Tingay) to have 'learned the game by making a fourth with three brothers'. Lenglen's advantage over the champion she unseated in 1919 was not only that she had recently competed (against women), a sharpening denied to her opponent because in those days reigning champions sat out the tournament until the challenge round, but that she had recently practised with men.

By the Thirties, top women regularly practised with top or near-top men, and there was no more individual advantage to be gained. At that point what becomes fascinating are the advantages that were, apparently deliberately, *not* gained.

Dorothy Round, who won her first Wimbledon singles in 1934, used to practise with men in Birmingham in their lunch-hour and (as quoted by Gwen Robyns) found one in particular 'most helpful as he played a bit like a woman. He played from the baseline and didn't rush up to the net'. This tallies with Dan Maskell's account (quoted by the same writer) of his practice games with Helen Wills Moody. She required of him two sets in which he was to 'play like a very good woman player'. Then there was a third set, in which he might play as himself. (True to the adage, he beat her in both styles.) The third set she regarded not as useful practice but merely as fun for both players.

In these accounts there is a perceptible hint that both those champions of the Thirties possessed aptitudes for a more flexible type of tennis which they could have developed by playing against men, but which they chose not to develop, because they would have been of no use in competition against women. It becomes thinkable that, by the Seventies, women's tennis has learnt all it can (including how to 'rush up to the net') from practice matches with men and won't make its next advance until it breaks the last inhibition (and ceases to be women's tennis) by competing against men.

There was some public sympathy last year for the idea that the women players are entitled to an equal share of the Wimbledon prize money because they play equally entertaining tennis. The argument is, however, too shaky to rely on, since it could cut the ground from under the whole idea of competing for prizes at all. A player knocked out in the first round might be able to enter a wholly just claim to have played more entertaining and more crowd-pleasing tennis than the champion. Meanwhile the arguments against equal pay are, at least for the time being, irrefutable. The women don't play best-of-five matches (though they used to, in the U.S. championships, from 1894 to 1901) and they don't play through either as large a quantity or as high a quality of opposition. There is only one complete answer they could make: to enter open (bisexual) competition.

The day they first did so, they would, of course, be wiped out. But so was the (male) opposition when the 'cannonball' service was introduced in 1912, and again when the full power game was introduced in the Twenties, and yet again when it was re-introduced after the Second World War. In those cases, the opposition proved to have been wiped out only until it had time to learn either to copy the new style or to devise substitutes that could score as many points. Women's tennis would certainly not be able to learn as quickly, since it is a whole tennis generation's mental and playing habits that would have to be unlearnt and re-formed; and there is no guarantee it could learn at all.

If you compare players within the same sex (whichever sex), it is manifest that a good big 'un doesn't always beat a good little 'un. Tennis seems infinitely fertile of skills that can sutstitute for muscle and reach. This is a prima facie reason, though no more, for suspecting that size and strength (which, in comparisons between the sexes, are anyway a matter of averages, not individuals) are less critical in tennis than they seem to be in athletics. Again, the improvement wrought in the play of stay-at-home amateurs when they enter inter- national professional competition suggests that any player's game is partly formed by the standard of the opposition and that talent can be stretched by meeting better-quality opposi- tion. Even so, there might be an absolute limit beyond which the talent and power of a whole sex, like those of any par- ticular individual, just won't stretch. No one can tell (though anyone can guess) until it is put to the test.

Given that many incomes would be at risk and that much interesting tennis would be obscured while the women's game went into what might not prove a merely temporary eclipse, it would not be dishonourable if the women players refused the test and continued to develop their own game in its separate (and justly lower-paid) compartment. But there would always remain the untested possibility that separate development meant truncated development. Suppose Helen Wills Moody could have been an even better player than she was? It doesn't come graciously from someone shielded from personal challenge not only, now, by middle age but by lifelong lack of talent, yet something in me keeps feeling: 'Go on. I dare you.'

Lyric Tennis

(Spectator, 1978)

The trouble with going to Wimbledon is that you miss so much of the tennis. It's thought to be television that has brought in the crowds. As a result, the only place where you can now be sure of seeing a match is at home, on television. In my teens I watched the 1948 men's singles final from a second-row bench without really trying — without debenture, clout or queueing, just by arriving a bit early. That would now be as deep in day-dreamland as winning the title. On the other hand, the All England Club is much nicer to visit now than then. The ivy-infested Centre Court still disputes with Glyndebourne the claim to be the ugliest edifice open to the public in England, but since the game went pro the spectators have gone prole, to the vast improvement of manners and ambience. No more social aggressors demonstrating they Know Their Way Around; just patient family outings, beer and ice cream.

At home, unless you forego the score-calling and the distinctive noises of net-cords and mis-hits, you have to leave the sound turned up, which means you get the commentary. Goodness knows why television assumes tennis needs commentary. Spectators at Wimbledon manage to see a sizzling crosscourt return without being told that that's what they've just seen. Why shouldn't televiewers? It may be professional envy that makes commentators so governessy about poor Ilie Nastase. His talents obviously include a natural turn for delivering commentary on matches while he plays them. This year Dan Maskell affronted syntax as usual ('That gives he and his partner break point') and seemed to pass on his ineptitude with words to the papers, more than one of which described Martina Navratilova as a Czech 'expatriot'. The introduction

131

of Mark Cox to the microphone produced a new vocabulary of surrealism. A breeze on court, he remarked from experience, 'can throw your service out of Limbo'. (Perhaps the Prince of Wales will pursue the doctrinal point.)

This year Jimmy Connors changed the grunt that used to accompany his service into a hiss like the air brakes on a heavy goods vehicle; and Nastase presented to the public a front face unexpectedly resembling the Turin Shroud, after joining Bjorn Borg in a resolve to pass through the championships unshaven. Perhaps they were proving that a tournament is a tourney and the contestants still subject to the vows and vigils of chivalry. Perhaps they were just shewing that, although, by pleading their entertainment value, the women have got their prize money increased, there are in fact still some entertaining games women can't play.

In fact the women were still the victims of minor prejudice. Evonne Goolagong has spoken up or, rather, by using her maiden name in the USA, gestured up against Wimbledon's insistence on changing a woman player's playing name if she marries in mid-career. That had made Ms Goolagong into one of two Mrs Cawleys in the tournament, but it is the practice in general, not just the flukes, that needs remedy. Now the players are paid, there is no excuse for denying them the freedom given to professional actresses and writers. This anachronism, I expect, will vanish pretty soon, if only because it's commercial nonsense to hazard brand loyalties by re-naming the brand. Another happening, however, put me in mind of 1975, when Arthur Ashe was acclaimed as the first Black to win Wimbledon, quite as though it hadn't been won in 1957 and 1958, by Althea Gibson. This year paragraphs gushed about how Borg might, might not and finally did equal Fred Perry's record (since the abolition of the challenge round) of three singles titles in a row, but no one spared a sentence to say that that supposedly unique feat had already been performed by *three* women (Helen Wills, Louise Brough and Maureen Connolly).

It was a year when service return often prevailed over service, and lyric over heroic tennis. Much thought had clearly been given, out on the circuits, to how to circumvent the heavy servers, and I suspect that, when Wimbledon fort-

132

night arrived, the unsunbaked grass helped the counter attack. The result was Tom Okker intelligently running in under the guns of that stately Argentine galleon Guillermo Vilas: the best demonstration of playing the opponent, as distinct from playing one's own game and succeeding or failing according to how fluently it's going, since the final where Ashe had studied how Connors might be defeated and, by taking thought, defeated him. Okker next sang his duet with Nastase. The delight then was that each played his own game and it was the same game.

Against Borg, however, neither thought nor power could prevail. Borg carried both light and heavy armament, and has made himself the master of all modes as of all surfaces. The one thing he doesn't yet do is catch the imagination. I made a correct prediction of both singles champions this year, but in Borg's case I uttered it with the same *hélas* that I find myself appending to my opinion that he is the finest player certainly since the war and quite concievably since the game began. He plays clever, original, imaginative tennis. Yet, as you watch, the heart won't take fire. It's like listening to brilliant and witty dialogue spoken in a flat voice.

Ms Navratilova, by contrast, has considerable power over a spectator's heart, including that of drawing it into the mouth. Her semi-final with Ms Goolagong afforded the purest pleasure lyric tennis can give. Even her final, though seldom lovely tennis, was a much more intellectually and emotionally engaging contest than finals usually are. As a match player, she has only two disabilities. She won't make an ungainly stroke, even when nothing else will do; and she'd sooner forfeit the point than play a banal, merely bread-and-butter shot. She and Nastase are players of the (to my taste) most exciting kind, because they are always in danger of losing through sheer talent.

133

Baroque-'n'-Roll

Baroque – 'n' – Roll

(Written in 1986 for this collection, with the incorporation of fragments of a lecture and of a radio talk delivered in the 1960s. In quoting Marvell in the opening section I have, for the reader's ease, modernised spelling and capitalisation although the earlier versions, reproduced in, for instance, the Five Poems *published by J. L. Carr, are, to my taste, much more pleasing.)*

1

Now therefore ...

You can compose a concerto or write one, build a basilica or compose one. Form is the constant throughout the arts.

When you read Andrew Marvell's indeed marvellous *To His Coy Mistress*, it makes no difference to your enjoyment and only peripheral comment on your perception whether you simply take in the poem's construction in three quasi-paragraphs or whether it puts you in mind of the experience of casting your eye up a façade (of, say, a 17th-century town house) whose three storeys stand in the relation to one another 10:6:7 (the proportions in fact of the paragraphs of the poem) or whether you liken the poem to a concerto with a longish first movement and briefer second and third movements.

A structure can be transposed from one art to another and the only obligatory changes will be those enforced by the difference of the (in the more or less literal sense) material.

For an analogy with Marvell's poem you would probably do better (that is, come closer) with a work of music than of architecture. Music and literature both make structural use of tempo, but architecture deploys tempo only as a subaltern to its use of space, though it commands a thousand metaphorical and indirect methods of acceleration and decelaration.

What I cite as the proportions of Marvell's three paragraphs is a blunt instrument fashioned by reducing, in the way you reduce fractions, the crude line-count of each paragraph. It *seems* just, since the metre is the same, with the same number of stresses to each line, all through the poem. Yet such a count of lines is as crass as it would be to determine the relation between the three movements of a concerto by totting up the number of bars in each, a procedure that takes no account of the composer's having marked some movements and, indeed, some passages within a movement to be played fast and others slowly, let alone of the tonal relation between one key and another.

I sometimes entertain a hope that it might help to diminish the unjust intellectual disesteem of literature were novelists and poets invited to equip their books with structural analyses of the kind that were, during my adolescence in the 1940s, prefaced to (or in pamphlet format used to fall out of) miniature scores. I do not believe, however, that that would perform the service literature so badly needs even could you dissuade busy writers from so far emulating the music-analysts as to set down great chunks of their work as 'bridge-passages'.

When not driven to that refuge, the music-analysts loved, above all, 'sonata form'. On their happiest days they could, by disentangling themes into the shape A-B-A, produce from, say, a concerto three movements each of which consisted of, as it were, three continuous movements. In concert halls and on gramophone records the analysis was, however, regularly given the lie — and the composer more disgracefully so — by the horrid habit of amputating the second performance of a passage the composer marked to be repeated, from the beginning or from a designated sign, after the performance of an intervening stretch. When it was an aria that was in question, the excision was virtually invariably made. It transformed an A-B-A structure into A-B, and it robbed the composer of one of the simplest and often most moving effects he can produce in an audience, namely the experience of emotions proper to Ulysses (whether Homer's or Monteverdi's) when he at last achieves his return home.

I put no faith in the efficacy of literary analyses because it was not the expectations provoked in audiences by musical analyses that eradicated savage amputations from performances of music. It is thanks to the renaissance of baroque music and of, at least by intention, authentic performance that such amputations are now virtually banished from platforms and opera houses. The worst that is likely to befall you nowadays is that when theme A makes its return it will do so under such intense decoration of musical barbola-work that you will scarcely recognise it as theme A.

Unlike a concerto on the three-movement pattern that became established about a century after Marvell's death and that dominated the 19th century, Marvell's poem opens with the slow movement. Marvell makes his first poetic paragraph slow by literary methods: the meaning of what he says; and the drawing out of syllables by long vowel sounds and liquid alliterations which the tongue has to wade sweetly but slowly through. 'We would sit down and think which way/To walk and pass our long love's day.' 'My vegetable love should grow/Vaster than empires and more slow.'

The second movement begins with a mighty bang of brass and percussion: 'But at my back I always hear/Time's winged chariot hurrying near'. Abiding by the poem's constant metre, Marvell accelerates it and renders it choppy by both meaning and sound. The lines hurry because the chariot is hurrying; and the two *i* sounds of 'rry-ing' are crammed into a space where a more tranquil use of the same fast speed would make room for only one. The haste is the haste of anxiety.

The musical twin to Marvell's second paragraph is vocal and liturgical or, in oratorio, 'sacred': a *Dies Irae* or a God-mocking chorus such as the one in Handel's *Messiah*, 'He trusted in God that he would deliver him; let him deliver him if he delight in him.' Marvell also uses a counterpart to the device in earlier-than-Handel liturgical music whereby the composer makes a metaphor of the anguish of the Christian crucifixion by gathering the voices of his consort into a dissonance on 'crux' or on the first syllable of its grammatical metamorphoses 'crucem' and 'crucis'. Marvell's equivalent is a rhyme which, though sanctioned by the usage of verse in English, is marginally out-of-tune to the ear. Of rhymes of that

139

kind there is only one in the first paragraph of the poem, 'would' and 'Flood', which may in any case not have seemed an untrue rhyme to the ear of Marvell or his audience. In the last paragraph there is none. In the choppy middle paragraph there are two — or, strictly, two occurrences of the same quasi-rhyme; and only two lines separate them. One quasi-rhyme pre-echoes the other; and both are stringently reinforced by the meaning. The cosmically terrifying couplet 'And yonder all before us lie/Deserts of vast eternity' pre-echoes the most shocking half-a-line plus line in literature, the crux indeed of the poem, 'then worms shall try/That long preserv'd virginity'.

It is on a dissonance of grammar that the middle paragraph ends, a matching piece to the startling bang that opened it. This time the dissonance is not sanctioned except by the sense and by the unanswerable question of what else the poet could have done. Certainly it is conscious and deliberate. 'None' is manifestly a contraction of 'no one', in which the 'one' is manifestly, virtually punningly, a singular. To link it with the plural form of a verb endorses and is endorsed by meaning. The dissonance marks the two-in-oneness of embraced lovers, the singular duality of what is called in *Othello* the beast with two backs:

> The grave's a fine and private place
> But none I think do there embrace.

The final paragraph moves the poem into its true allegro. It has shed anxiety because the lovers have assumed the initiative. No longer liable to be overtaken by the winged chariot in its ungainly hurry, they can now impose on the sun, their natural clock, an equally rapid but much more dignified action: 'we will make him run.'

The perfect and perfectly rhymed couplets of the final paragraph work out the resolution of the discords that precede it. The deathly phallic image of the worms is answered by the lively phallic image in which the lovers will 'tear our pleasures with rough strife/Thorough the iron gates of life'.

In the colloquial sense, too, the last paragraph of the poem makes a triumphant resolution. The lover-poet (who may, of course, be more of a fictitious than of a directly autobiographical person) resolves that the woman, who wants to ('thy willing soul transpires'), indeed shall go to bed with him. She will be vanquished by the force of the argument which the poem in its entirety constitutes.

Marvell's quasi-musical devices are probably not conscious borrowings and almost certainly not deliberate adaptations. Rather, they are spontaneous counterparts developed for similar artistic purposes. After all, the music of great poetry is essentially poetic.

Yet there is a model, of which I am convinced Marvell was cogently aware, for his poem-argument in three phases. It is as though his poem has tried to swallow the model and use it as a metaphor but has been swallowed by the metaphor. The poem *is* what it is a metaphor of.

The model is one that sets out an argument in three propositions, constituting two premisses and the conclusion.

In the first mood of the first figure, an argument by syllogism is symbolically written:

$$\begin{array}{l} \text{MaP} \\ \underline{\text{SaM}} \\ \text{SaP.} \end{array}$$

M represents the Middle Term, which is invoked only to bring S and P, the Subject and Predicate Terms of the ultimate conclusion, into a valid relation to one another.

The premiss that contains P is, of the two premisses, the major premiss. It is from here that Marvell takes the proportions and some of the tempo of the three paragraphs of his poem: a major and universally applicable first paragraph; a swift and necessary to the argument but shorter second paragraph; and a shortish, rapidly and inevitably drawn paragraph of conclusion.

In full academic dress each of the Terms, S, P and M, bears over its head a bar or a saucer, which represents whether the Term is 'distributed' of 'undistributed'. It is amusing and apt that formal logic makes use of the same symbolic marks as those by which the scansion of verses in Latin and ancient Greek differentiates a long from a short syllable.

141

Fleshed in an example of the same syllogistic mood, the paradigm becomes

> All humans are sexual beings:
> We are humans:
> Therefore: — We are sexual beings.

Marvell declares the final paragraph of his poem to be the conclusion of a syllogism by introducing it with 'therefore': 'Now therefore, while the youthful hue' . . .

The validity and the formality of his poem-argument are those of great poetry and not of logic. Yet by the metaphor, which is an act of poetry, that makes his poem a syllogism he purloins the prestige and the ungainsayableness of the form of rational argument that has dominated the intellect of Europe since Aristotle discovered or invented it in the three hundreds B.C. The poem's conclusion brings two people intead of two Terms into a relationship. The necessity that will rapidly but without anxiety or hurry triumph over the woman's doubt and scruples is logical necessity.

2

(Meta)physics

English is a language which can barely open its mouth without uttering a metaphor.

In that, it differs considerably from French and vehemently from ancient Greek. In the literary, though not in the literal, sense there are great writers in both languages who are untranslatable into English. The literary tragedy of the Victorian age is that Britain was ruled by a class whose male children were taught Latin and Greek almost exclusively and whose scholars were word-and-emendation perfect in Greek but whose translators betray the utter deafness of their civilisation to the tone of the literature it considered classical. A generation was brought up not on Homer but on the aptly named travesty of him by Butcher and Lang.

Greek is an essentially kinetic language, doing as much as possible of its work through its verbs. It has a big vocabulary

142

of prepositions, which bring the kinetic force of the verb to bear on the nouns over which the preposition exerts its magnetic field and which can also impart direction to a verb by compounding with its beginning, sometimes in twos like carriages building a train, though a preposition can also disjoin itself from a compound verb and stand in isolation as it may in English, creating a difference as idiomatic as that between 'stand with them' and 'withstand them'.

The constant directional indicators in Greek are, however, the particles, which so far as I know have no equivalent in other languages: unstressed and usually monosyllabic words that are cast into a sentence or phrase, where as a rule they stand in the position of the second word, and whose function is to state the relationship between this sentence and that or between this part and that of a single sentence. Some go bluntly and too conspicuously into English as 'for' or 'with the result that' and others clamour to be left out of translation. Greek cannot, however, be idiomatically or even correctly written without them. It is a language that cannot juxtapose statements without tossing into one or both the statements in question a particle that almost mutely indicates whether the second statement explains, amplifies, results from or is co-equal with the first.

Thanks to the particles, every passage of Greek prose or verse contains its own structural analysis. The analysis is conducted, almost *sotto voce*, in the interstices of what it is analysing. Reading Greek is like reading the score and the commentary of the music-analyst simultaneously.

The analysis which the particles perform while a passage of Greek continues to its narrative, poetic or, indeed, analytic end is a matter of singling out and categorising small, line-to-line relationships. I conceive but I am not so convinced as to advance it as a thesis that it was the training in picking out relationships which the language administered by its nature and which its readers absorbed without noticing what they were about that allowed Greek writers to rely so trustingly on their readers' understanding of relationships as to create their works in terms of naked and uncushioned relationships alone. Sappho (whose Greek does not lack particles) is a lyric poet whose poems lack padding to the same extent as Japanese poems in translation. The dramas of the great Greek dramatists dare to set on the stage *dramatis personae* held in being by the relationships they are part of and dramatic action consisting of the development of those relationships.

From Aristotle's analysis of Greek drama it is the *Oedipus the King* of Sophocles that emerges as the hero. The dramatic idiom of Euripides is more difficult for a modern to understand and was perhaps so for Aristotle. Euripides had to wait for a new era to achieve full understanding. In the 17th century of the new era his *Hyppolytus* was so seamlessly metamorphosed by Jean Racine into *Phèdre* that it is impertinent to speak of metamorphosis. It seems simpler to conceive that Racine and Euripides were a single superb dramatic poet who had two native languages and lived two thousand years.

For rendering neither Racine nor Greek drama has the English-speaking theatre devised an idiom — of language or of presentation; and the people who mount its plays go in super-stitious dread that an audience , if left alone with a drama of relationships, would feel itself trapped by or impaled on the acute angles the drama creates.

Yet a number of poets in English, Marvell among them, did — and, though with results nothing like Racine's, did during the 17th century — tease a poetry of relationships out of the in-herent turn of the English language for metaphor. The metaphors thus wrought are often technological processes, which already encapsulate a relationship between practical actions and theory. Our practice in working computers should by now have instructed us all over again in the taste for the 17th-century poetry bizarrely called metaphysical.

The metaphor that absorbs one of Marvell's poems is the technique of syllogism, which consists of both performing actions and understanding and applying the rules. In *The Definition of Love*, in whose title the verbal noun 'definition' incarnates the dual nature of metaphysical poetry, juxtaposed verses metaphor the lovers' love in the projection of maps onto a globe ('Be cramp'd into a planisphere') and in the projection by mathematical theory of parallel lines into infinity ('But ours so truly parallel/Though infinite can never meet').

William Shakespeare, whose sonnets are, I am convinced, among the early examples and the most potent exemplars of the metaphysical mode, begins a sonnet in the bureaucratic and legalistic territory of the forbidding of the banns of marriage ('Let me not to the marriage of true minds/Admit impediments') and in his next quatrain flips the metaphor with the deftness of a pancake cook into the theory and practice of navigation at sea by dead reckoning ('It is the star of every wandering bark/Whose worth's unknown although his height be taken').

From their molten metaphors the metaphysical poets draw out filigree. They construct it into designs that are also definitions which are also diagrams. The process is as beautiful as the product. The poem becomes a rebus of itself.

The name 'metaphysical' was affixed to certain poets of the 17th century in the 18th: by Dr Johnson. It stuck thanks to Johnson's prestige. Yet since 'metaphysics' is, in modern English both then and now, a speculative area of philosophy, it was a curious name for someone whose prestige was chiefly that of a lexicographer to apply to poets whose preferred metaphors were practical and material.

In the introduction to her Penguin selection, of 1957, *The Metaphysical Poets*, Helen Gardner unravelled part of the puzzle by finding that Samuel Johnson was alluding to a remark made before the 17th century was out by John Dryden. She quotes Dryden's statement that John Donne 'affects the metaphysics' not only in his satires but in his love poems 'and perplexes the minds of the fair sex with nice speculations of philosophy'.

The puzzle can be taken, I think, a touch further. In the 17th century, as Dryden well knew from the instance of Aphra Behn, a woman might be a literary genius and women as a class might be literate. No doubt they were already, as a class, what they conspicuously became in the 18th century and remain till this day, namely great readers. The opportunity was afforded, I imagine, not by any superior literary bent but by the fact that reading, unlike writing or 'study', does not demand an advance pledge of uninterrupted time for doing it in but can be continued piecemeal in the intervals of conducting, whether by one's own bodily work or by the organisation of other people's, a household. Civilisation must have often been saved by the simplest technological device, the bookmark.

In one sense, however, a woman, whether of general literacy or of commanding literary power, will have seemed to Dryden, and scarcely less to Johnson, largely uneducated in the most classic sense. Women were seldom taught Latin and rarely Greek. They were, so to speak, expected to know the meaning but not the etymology of 'metaphysics'. In using the word in connexion with the practical metaphors of Donne and Abraham Cowley, Dryden was, I suspect, wrapping up a joke about the most bizarre of all Greek etymologies, which hinges on a sense, though not a logical one, in which the speculative does follow from the practical. He was declaring, I conceive, his belief that it is by a bizarre process that metaphysical poets cause love to follow from the workings of sextants or astrolabes.

'Metaphysical' is something between a word without etymology and a word without meaning, though it is not without history. Its components are meta, one of whose meanings is 'after', and phusikos, 'natural'. The Greek letter phi was regularly transliterated into Latin, and therefore usually into English, as ph, and the Greek u as y. The two Greek components of 'metaphysical' were not hitched, as happens with some scientific names, by a modern hand. Yet neither did they unite to create an ordinary word in ancient Greek.

When Aristotle addressed his uniquely analytic plus encyclopaedic intellect to subjects that included space, time, generation, corruption and weather, his treatises were naturally accorded the comprehensive title ta phusika, 'the natural things'. Keeping the plural of the Greek neuter plural adjective but giving it an English form, the English language eventually acquired both the word 'physics' and its usual title in translation for Aristotle's book. Whether his enquiries into speculative philosophy followed those into natural phenomena in Aristotle's oeuvre or whether his work on truth, being and knowledge simply followed his work on 'the natural things' into the library of his works, Aristotle's editors (according to the account in the 1940 revision of the 1937 Oxford Companion to Classical Literature) gave his philosophical treatise the title 'after the "physics"', meta ta phusica. That near-accident is all the pedigree 'metaphysics' and 'metaphysical' have.

146

When English poets of the 17th century spun filigree metaphors from natural and technical processes, it may well have seemed to Dryden and to Johnson after him that the poets had as strong and quite as logical a claim to the word 'metaphysical' as metaphysicians have.

3

To Saint Teresa

Local, specialised and determinate in time, metaphysical poetry is nevertheless part of the great full-blown peony, the baroque, which opened in all parts of Europe a little before the 17th century and which, in the 18th, pushed its petals further apart, admitting space, and became the transfixed *feu d'artifice* of the rococo, both of them still, towards the end of the 20th century, in valid and vivid bloom.

With an internationalism apt to the styles, 'baroque' is a word that English uses in its French form and 'rococo' is said to be a fancy Italianate form of the French 'rocaille', which alludes to the shell-decoration of grottoes. The styles were current in Britain from long before but their names did not become so until the first half of the 19th century; and then they were used as often by way of insult as of description.

It would be pleasing to compensate them by using them now purely as praise and by affixing them to every great artist who is an historically plausible candidate, but it would not work. Racine himself is not, to my judgement, a baroque artist. Neither — quite — is Nicolas Poussin. The paintings of G. B. Tiepolo employ devices and motifs both baroque and rococo but are of their own (great) genus. I think the same is true of the works of Sir Christopher Wren. Of the incomparable composers, G. F. Handel is almost always baroque, W. A. Mozart himself alone. Mozart is most nearly baroque in *Idomeneo* and *Don Giovanni*, I imagine because the themes of and the circumstances in which he composed those operas most cogently provoked the major ambivalence of his emotions, that towards his father.

Ronald Firbank did not become, to a literary ear, recognisably himself until he had with flair and hard work fashioned a modern rococo prose. In it he couched *Vainglory*, which he published in 1915; into it he adopted and adapted practices borrowed, consciously, from jazz, the great musical rococo contemporary with him; he deepened and solidified his idiom into the baroque masterpiece *Concerning the Eccentricities of Cardinal Pirelli*, which he published (posthumously, by just over a month) in 1926. An artist of different temperament and perhaps fewer contretemps with his period, John Milton vaults styles. Milton is a great every kind of poet, including (witness Helen Gardner's selection) a metaphysical, and the author of three great baroque poetic monuments, the *Ode on the Morning of Christ's Nativity*, *Comus* and *Lycidas*.

Likewise John Nash is a graceful and commanding architect in what cannot be called the classical manner because that is a classic muddle-word when it is meant to mean more than 'acquainted with Greek and Latin' who, between 1815 and 1821, to the commission of the Prince Regent who became George IV in 1820, imparted its final and definitive form to the much worked-over Royal Pavilion at Brighton and, two centuries after Sir John Vanbrugh built Blenheim Palace, gave the British Isles a second incomparable monument of architectural baroque.

Towards the other extreme of the 19th century Aubrey Beardsley was born and educated at Brighton, and the convoluted shape of the Pavilion fell across his development. He died at the age of 25 in 1898, the creator of pictures (pictures indeed, though, contrary to the fashion or the pretensions of the time, designed to be seen printed, in black and white or another single colour, on the pages of volumes or on surfaces where posters were stuck) in the manners of Japonaiserie, neo-Gothic and baroque. The initial V, in his designs for an edition of Ben Jonson's *Volpone*, uses the most baroque, bizarre and tragic of animals, an elephant, to the same artistic purpose as the obelisk-bearing sculptural elephant executed by another hand but designed by Gian Lorenzo Bernini in the 1660s for the Piazza Santa Maria sopra Minerva in Rome. Messalina, in *Messalina returning from the bath*, is set by Beardsley to stamp sinisterly up the cardinal motif of baroque architecture, an external staircase, but the curve and sweep of staircases in the baroque is transposed by Beardsley into the bare breasts and bunched-up skirts of Messalina. *Chopin Ballade* transposes into a picture a quintessential of baroque sculpture, a prancing equestrian statue.

Why, apart from Beardsley's personal taste and his mother's ambition that he should prove a child-prodigy pianist, Chopin for baroquestrianism? I think Beardsley had recognised that self-contained, half romantic pocket of baroque, created, about 1820 to 1830, by Frédéric Chopin, Felix Mendelssohn and Vincenzo Bellini, without or with (with chiefly in *Oberon* and the Konzertstück, op. 79) a composer of whom Beardsley made an imaginary portrait, C. M. von Weber. Often by the device of retarding and elongating the melodic line, which is sometimes a vocal line, almost beyond bearing, they re-work melody into filigree and are music's metaphysical poets.

The title of Milton's baroque *Ode* probably, I think, reflects a Puritan avoidance of the word 'Christmas'; but the poem is the opposite of puritanical. The march of the long lines and the regular flurries of the shorter lines describe a shape as grand and as decorative as a baroque cartouche. The baby the poem celebrates has two paternal lineages, mutually exclusive yet both supposedly vouched for by scripture (a state of affairs papered over by laborious exegesis). It is 'the heaven-born child' who provokes 'awe'. Yet it is the royal descendant who gives form to the metaphysical metaphor that turns the December deciduousness of trees (at least in the northern hemisphere) into, for all the femaleness of 'Nature', the masculine gesture of feudal obeissance, the sweeping off of one's hat: 'Nature in awe to him/Had doffed her gaudy trim/With her great master so to sympathise.'

Baroque is an open, sometimes an explosive embrace of contradictions and oppositions, intellectual and of feeling. Ambiguity and puns are its raw material merely. Its essence is the ambivalence, in full deep psychoanalytic import, of emotions. It is a pair of giant curly brackets that clip together things irreconcilable.

Its bold embrace encompasses images devoid of dignity: comic images; domestic images; the taken literally imagist content of religious myths; images of such bodily secretions as tears and milk. Richard Crashaw's great poem *The Weeper* unites the repentant tears of Saint Mary Magdalen with the

149

hunger of a baby, even a baby angel, for a product of a female body: 'Every morn from hence/A brisk cherub something sips' (where the 'brisk' has the same unexpected and bracing unpretentiousness as Milton's 'doffed' and 'trim'), with the result that 'his song/Tastes of his breakfast all day long'. In the 1570s Tintoretto (Jacopo Robusti) squirted the product of Juno's lactating breast round the firmament in his painting, now in the National Gallery, *The Origin of the Milky Way*, a tale taken from G. Julius Hyginus, the turn-of-BC/AD friend, fellow Latin writer and fellow myth-collector of Ovid (P. Ovidius Naso).

The most moved and moving account of the execution of the king Charles I is delivered in a domestic metaphor, by a parliamentarian, Andrew Marvell, MP for Hull: 'But bow'd his comely head/Down as upon a bed'.

Baroque painters, sculptors and stuccoists invoke ceiling and walls to make a metaphor of the interplay between earth and a mythical heaven. The same interplay is created by dramatic composers and their stage designers and producers who could produce a god from a descending machine. In the operatic and erotic masterpiece, *L'Incoronazione di Poppaea*, which he composed in his old age, Claudio Monteverdi accepts the comedic flexibility afforded by two facts: despite the pretensions to continuity of the Holy Roman Empire, the dynasty of his hero, the emperor Nero, was no longer a political and threatening power; and the inhabitants of his supernatural stratum, though all even half-educated people were still instructed in their names and stories, were no longer the personages of a believed-in religion. Yet Monteverdi's church music is no less baroque and no less comedic. He takes advantage of the convenient translated text from the Song of Solomon, 'Nigra sum sed formosa', 'I am black but comely', to throw into his 1610 *Vespers of the Virgin* an early declaration that black is beautiful as psychologically sympathetic and as sophisticatedly aware of the bizarrerie as the studies of black men by P. P. Rubens; and in his motet 'Currite populi', published in 1625, he sketches an almost farcical musical onomatopoeia of scurrying people.

Likewise, madonnas in Counter-Reformation baroque paintings are assumed to heaven in the upright stance of a soldier on guard duty or a firework rocket. Often they disdain underfoot the crescent moon as though it were the top rung of a ladder they no longer need. In *The Ascension of Saint Rose of Lima* Beardsley sends up a pair of rockets or holy females, saint and madonna, held together by their loving and possibly homosexual arms about one another.

All the ambivalences of the baroque are reduplications of the inescapable ambivalence at the heart of human consciousness: the knowledge that this impressively powerful, potent or desirable human flesh is mortal; and the knowledge that the orgasm that satisfies desire will, temporarily but signally, do desire to death.

Awareness of both halves of both ambivalences dictates the form of one of the metaphysical sonnets (64) of Shakespeare, which unites the two ambivalences by the punning use of 'my love' to signify both 'this person whom I love' and 'my desire for this person': 'Ruin hath taught me thus to ruminate/That time will come and take my love away./This thought is as a death which cannot choose/But weep to have that which it fears to lose.'

In a sense the central artefact of the baroque is a marble bed ('Nor in thy marble vault shall sound/My echoing song'), where lovers sleep together 'But none I think do there embrace'.

In painting, the paintings of J. A. Watteau establish the central material of the rococo as silk, that material which has only to fall into a fold to be shot through, as though by a sad thought, by a colour not its own. In sculpture, as often in architecture, the quintessential substance of the baroque is marble, a material likely, like some types of cheese, to be veined by a counter-colour. When it is pure white it can, at the working of a master, simulate the various softnesses of hair, lace and flesh and yet it remains hard and cold. A natural rendering of the baroque ambivalence, it renders flesh at once desirable and in the clutch of rigor mortis.

In 1622 to 1625 Bernini, in a sculptural group commissioned by Cardinal Borghese and still in the Galleria Borghese at Rome, metamorphosed the inherent ambivalence of marble into the metaphorical ambivalence of metamorphosis itself.

The story of Daphne's paradoxical evasion of rape by the god Apollo he took from Ovid's collection in Latin verse of

Greek myths, which had been for centuries Europe's text-book of classical mythology under its Latinised-Greek title, Metamorphoses (morphe, 'form, shape, figure', plus meta in another of its meanings, one of those it assumed in compound words, with the significance of change of place or condition — or, in Sonnet 64, 'interchange of state').

As the pursuing Apollo is on the point of seizing her, the seeming simulacrum of Daphne's living flesh is blasted not by death but by her transformation into another living individual, of, however, another living but vegetable species. Her body's extremeties issue leafy twigs; her feet become roots. Apollo is left to cultivate, if he will, his 'vegetable love'. And Bernini has performed his miraculous metamorphosis of Latin verse into baroque sculpture in marble.

It was not, however, to Daphne, a discontinued personage so far as belief was concerned, that Bernini dedicated the baroque but, with the concurrence of Crashaw's metaphysical *Hymn* to her, to Saint Teresa of Ávila. He did so in one of the most astounding works of art in the world.

A small side-chapel (the Cornaro chapel) in a not huge urban church (Santa Maria della Vittoria, Rome) underwent between 1645 and 1652 metamorphosis into a silent opera house permanently displaying a spectacle which, in a symbolism too transparent to be refused or refuted by the most non- or anti-Freudian, consists of sexual intercourse.

In quasi-theatre boxes at the sides of the chapel, sculpted spectators in a mimicked architectural setting watch or ignore the spectacle. The visiting flesh-and-blood audience is architecturally directed to view it from the front, against the marble colours and patterns of the altar. The materials that create the illusion include natural top lighting as well as the gilded sun-rays represented by the baroque glory that spears downward like shafts of rain about the central figures. On the vaulted ceiling, painted angelic figures tumble about clouds composed of plaster. Howard Hibbard justly says in his 1965 Penguin volume on Bernini that it is as though one of them had descended to the earthly level of the altar and there become the three-dimensional marble figure of the angel in the central sculptural group, who stands and, holding it as fastidiously as a fork as a buffet supper, thrusts his spear into the heart of the other figure, Saint Teresa, who is falling backwards in rapture.

It is comedy, though not the comedy of scoffing or disbelief, that an often puritan religion that prized chastity should mount such a spectacle in a church.

The comedy was made possible by the metamorphosis of a deceased person into a saint. Saint Teresa, founder of the order of Discalced Carmelites and wielder of considerable bureaucratic and organisational authority in the church, died in 1582 and was (comparatively quickly by some saintly standards) canonised in 1622.

The rapturous fall backwards that Bernini turns into sculpture was reported by Saint Terersa in the literary form of autobiography. Should she be standing at the time of visitation by a vision, she fell backwards, transported and with body contracted. The golden spear, at whose iron tip there appeared to be a point of fire, was thrust into her heart by the hands of an angel and reached her entrails, which he seemed to pull out when he pulled out the spear, causing her so sweet a pain that she could not wish it to cease, and making her moan. (I am relying on J. M. Cohen's Penguin translation of Saint Teresa's Spanish.) The angel was, she says, not tall but short, his face aflame and transcendently beautiful. She classifies him as one of the cherubim, though anonymous to her. He is indeed one of the youthful angels who in Crashaw sips the Magdalen's tears. Bernini gives him the youth as well as the beauty attributed to him by Saint Teresa. He is just old enough for his sexual exercise.

Bernini's baroque lack of fear of the literal import of religious imagery poses with double point the question how a woman who had never experienced sexual intercourse could have such accurate knowledge of it and of the phenomena of erection. The answer, like the ultimate answer to the question how the church could permit the chapel to come into and remain in being, is: by virtue of the literary imagination.

Psychoanalysis dicloses the fantasised interpretations of sex that children often construct out of their ignorance, wishes and habit of thinking more logically than rationally. The literary imagination is in contrast to childish fantasy. It creates fictions that are often more accurate than factual reports are.

153

Most fictions are avowed, even vaunted fictions. Psychologically, though not literally, Saint Teresa's was not religious faith but what S. T. Coleridge called the 'poetic faith' constituted by 'the willing suspension of disbelief for the moment'. Saint Teresa was not in a position, however, where she could avow or admit, even to herself, the fictitious nature of her visions. They were built on subject-matter officially claimed to be the most important in the world, which in itself challenged scrutiny. The absolute truthfulness of her accounts of her visions had to pass the interrogation both of the ecclesiastical authorities and of her own conscience.

In disguise from both herself and the church Saint Teresa's autobiography was not the pattern of saintliness it passed for but a classic account of the pattern of the developing literary imagination. She and her near-contemporary Miguel de Cervantes personify Spanish devotion to literature.

Saint Teresa's literary nature was frustrated first in her childhood, by a father who forbade her to read novels, and then a second time, when she was an adult nun, by a father confessor who forbade her to read books in Spanish and confined her reading to Latin. She was already in the habit of conversing, inaudibly to others, with God. In a remark which, she records, she did not understand at the time, he promised her compensation in the form of a living book. She began to experience rapturous visions. From them she made a book indeed. Her visions were the product less of sexual than of literary frustration.

A small, pleasing component in the charm and comedy of the Cornaro Chapel is that it is a tribute by the visual arts — virtually all of them — to literature. Obliquely it is a requital for the many tributes that baroque literature pays to music. 'What passion cannot MUSICK raise and quell!' says Dryden's *Song for St Cecilia's Day, 1687* in celebration of the legendary patron of music; and he finishes the song with the splendidly musical explosion of baroque paradoxes 'The TRUMPET shall be heard on high,/The dead shall live, the living die,/And MUSICK shall untune the sky'.

The literary tributes to music are regularly turned or half turned back into music, a matter in which Handel was a specialist. He is as deep as Dryden in percussive baroque contrasts when he sets Dryden's great *Ode* in honour of Saint Cecilia's Day, *Alexander's Feast or the Power of Musique*. Matching musical to poetic lyricism, he sets Milton's *L'Allegro* and *Il Penseroso* (as well as *Il Moderato*, added in the 18th century's propensity for self-caricature) and accomplishes the wish Milton frames in *L'Allegro*: 'Lap me in soft Lydian airs/ Married to immortal verse'.

4

The Invention?

Architecture deploys neither the immediacy and decipherability of music in creating mood nor the representational power that painting and literature can deploy when they care to. Such deceptions as architecture commands are deceptions within its own architectural terms. Entasis swells columns outward in order to prevent them from *looking* out-of-true in the other direction. When a member that performs the architectural function of a column is made to resemble a woman and becomes a caryatid, it is sculpture, a sometimes representational art, and not architecture that makes the transformation.

Baroque architecture can invite you only to follow the geometrical spacial relationships of architecture in general, prompting you to ask: What bears the weight of this, props up that, gives rise to that? As architecture, it can astound and move you only by deploying space and size, including small size, and by associating shapes, whether of enclosed space or of outline, in juxtapositions you have not been led to expect — as it does when it associates a pediment with a dome. The dome, indeed, is its major element of emotion, a hemispherical space rising from a circle or a circle set in a rectangle and capable of roofing over a cubically enclosed space.

When the fashion for artificial ruins flickered through Europe during and immediately after the 18th century, architecture acquired through it some quasi-representational power: it became able to evoke literary, as it were historical responses; but it was not absolved of the practical duty peculiar to architecture, namely that it must stand up. You can build an apparently ruined wall, two thirds of the height your structure suggests it should be, and pretend that the top third,

155

which never in fact existed, has fallen off, but the two-thirds that you do build is under an obligation to stand up, just as your seemingly ruined roof is obliged to keep out the weather.

Painters can compose the baroque death-in-orgasm by flinging heroic or numinous bodies in tour-de-force foreshortening about canvas or the wall or ceiling that architects provide in place of canvas. The elements of the composition are convulsed as though by an explosion; the designer no longer seeks to balance one against another in a simulacrum of heavenly or geometric harmony; instead, he arrests and transfixes the explosion at the very point of disintegration.

Except when it cantilevers a projection and seems to suspend it, without external support, over a void, architecture is compelled by its practical obligations to compose its baroque explosions of purely architectural motifs, without real or at least without deliberate real disintegrations and with only very minor simulated disintegrations.

Painting, however, can depict both the violent destruction of a work of architecture and its slow lapse over centuries of use. Baroque as an idiom for the visual arts was, I believe, invented between 1556 and 1559 in a pair of paintings that depict, besides more conspicuous things, the slow lapse under the impact of time of an age-old architectural construction, by way of allusion, perhaps, to the pictures' architectural strategy of design.

The inventor was Titian (Tiziano Vecelli), who had several times before been on the verge of inventing the baroque, most notably in Bacchus's great joyful and athletic leap from his chariot in the *Bacchus and Ariadne* in the National Gallery.

When Titian despatched the paintings, finished, in 1559, he said he had been working on them for three years. When he finished them, he was himself in or verging on his eighties. (The date of his birth is unknown.) Some of their lethal ambivalence was probably dictated by the awareness that his own death could not be long distant and by the memory of the death, in the year in which he began the paintings, of his friend Pietro Aretino, the outspoken literary pornographer, author of the text to a volume of designs by Giulio Romano whose engraver was imprisoned for their obscenity. Aretino, whom Titian several times painted, usually in straight portraiture but once, in an *Ecce Homo*, as Pontius Pilate, died a sudden and deeply baroque death. It was said that he laughed so immoderately at a joke at dinner that he overbalanced his chair backwards and struck his head on a corner.

The patron for whom Titian produced the pictures was the son of Titian's patron and friend, the king of Spain and also Holy Roman Emperor, Charles V, who voluntarily abdicated in the year before Titian began the two paintings for his son and died while he was working on them.

Those threads concerning the inevitability of lapse and death led from Titian's own life and affections into the ambivalence of the two pictures. They were compounded by an ambivalence of a different kind in the unwritten requirements his patron pressed on him. The patron, when heir to the throne of Spain, married Mary Tudor, queen of England, became, on the death of the emperor, Philip II of Spain and eventually sent the Armada against England and Elizabeth I, the half-sister who succeeded his wife.

Philip was a haut prince, a high Catholic and highly sexed. From Titian he demanded religious paintings, which it needed only the skill and imagination of a great master to provide, and also what Titian called, in the Venetian tradition, 'poesie', poetries, whose subjects it was left to Titian to determine.

Titian habitually found subjects for *poesie* by reverting to the no longer literally credible world of classical mythology, which made a respectable and scholarly occasion for the depiction of female nudes. Titian was in fact required to provide erotic pictures — in the least crude of senses; it is not a phallus but a thrustingly phallic god who leaps from his chariot to penetrate the seclusion of Ariadne. Titian had already, five years before, sent Philip a pair of *poesie*, of which he explained that, since the forms (the nudes) were seen one from the front and the other from the back, the pair would make a pleasantly varied decoration for a *camerino*. The first of that pair, a *Danaë*, he sent to Spain, the second, because of Philip's forthcoming marriage, to London. Its subject was Venus and Adonis. Eventually Philip must have taken the painting back to Spain, where it is still in the Prado; but perhaps the memories, reports, associations with upper-class fashion and even, it may be, engravings that remained in London brushed Shakespeare.

157

The hot high-summeriness of the *Venus and Adonis* is already thundery. The picture's perfect evocation of sex contains, by means of the mythological story, the presages of Adonis's death.

Philip was addressed in letters, including those Titian wrote him in courtly Italian, as 'most invincible Catholic king'. Spanish courtiers ended theirs: 'I kiss your royal feet and hands.' Titian, possibly because he was accustomed to living in the Venetian Republic or possibly because Philip's father had treated him as an equal, omitted the formula or omitted the feet and wrote: 'I kiss your Royal and Catholic hand'.

The more pious and Counter-Reformation and the more hung about with worldly titles the patron became, the less possible was it to design him openly aphrodisiac paintings but the more urgent his lust for painted flesh. The pair of *poesie* Titian sent him in 1559 have subjects that are kinky and that are netted about with the threads of death.

The paintings belong to the Duke of Sutherland and are (1986) on loan to the National Gallery of Scotland in Edinburgh. Both are built on stories from Ovid, the ancient world's combination of Sir James Frazer and Krafft-Ebing. They are separate stories, from Book II and Book III of the *Metamorphoses*, but the heroine of both is the blood-sporting and militantly virginal goddess Artemis or Diana, the moon deity whom Ben Jonson addressed, in *Cynthia's Revels*, with stately lyricism: 'Queen and huntress, chaste and fair.'

In each picture Titian isolates the high dramatic moment of a confrontation with the goddess that is destined to lead, after the moment of the picture, to a metamorphosis and a death.

Both pictures concern the band of athletic nymphs who accompany the goddess in her hunts against animals. Sweat is a bodily secretion of the kind that fashions metaphysical poetry; the need that Diana and her gang have for frequent baths furnished Titian with a pretext for multiple female nudity.

One of the nymphs, Callisto, has broken the gang's rule of chastity by being seduced by Jupiter. Ovid, a sly pornographer himself, makes Jupiter's embrace acceptable to Callisto by having the god disguise himself as Diana, and Titian fulfils his patron's wishes by echoing Ovid's suggestion that Diana is

158

a kind of lesbian gym-teacher whose nymphs adore her. Callisto, seduced, is pregnant. The moment of the picture is the moment when, her pregnancy advanced, Callisto refuses to strip and take the communal bath of the athletes, for fear of disclosing her enlarged belly. Naked nymphs tear the clothes from her. Diana extends her arm and points an accusing forefinger at Callisto's belly.

The narrative threads lead out of the picture to Diana's expulsion of Callisto from the gang, Callisto's giving birth to a son whose father is Jupiter, which provokes the jealousy of Juno, who turns Callisto into a bear. Grown-up, her son hunts down the bear. Jupiter prevents matricide by transforming mother and son alike into stars, the Great and the Little Bear.

Titian places his confrontation in a pool or stream, edged by old, probably Roman masonry, the composition braced by a tall freestanding squared post to the left of the picture centre. The vertical of the post is not parallel to the edge of the picture. From the top of the post a cupid pours water from an up-ended urn into the pool, in token of the waters of childbirth. The rape that some of the nymphs commit on Callisto's clothes is duplicated in the storm that splits the sky and stands emblem of the reverse-rape, the splitting by the baby on its way out, which the lethal child is about to perform. Callisto's pregnant and exposed belly is on the point of dehiscence, like some huge, rounded fruit. Her fruitfulness, however, condemns her to death.

The imminent splitting apart of Callisto's belly is duplicated by the splitting apart of the ten nude female bodies in the picture. It is an entirely female picture, a picture of childbirth, an entirely dehiscent picture. The nymphs break apart, in and across the pool. Some hold Callisto; some support Diana and her accusation. Callisto's legs slide away towards the left of the picture; failingly implorant, her arm stretches towards Diana and is overmastered by the goddess's pointing arm. Her very belly seeming to turn towards Diana, Callisto falls, in front and to the left of the post, as though she, too, is a pillar but one that has fallen down.

In the other picture it is a man who violates the women's bath and, by virtue of Titian's composition, the monumental female body constituted by the posse of female nudes.

Actaeon, out hunting, raises his arm as he passes unknowingly the slung curtain that screens the women's bath. Accompanied by his leading hound, he halts and tries to draw back. He has already seen the goddess's nakedness. She confronts him across the pool. Her lapdog or yapdog confronts the hound. The nymphs display comic faces of horror and curiosity as they seek to cover their nudity or, in one case, half-hide behind a squared post or pillar.

On the face of the pillar, a stag's skull gives warning of Actaeon's death. In a moment Diana will stoop to the water and flick some onto Actaeon's face, bidding him go and, if he can, recount his glimpse of her nudity. By that lethal baptism she will accomplish his metamorphosis into a stag, who, deprived of human speech, cannot call off his hounds when they hunt and kill him.

The architecture about and in the pool is more elaborate than in the *Callisto*, arched as well as pillared. In the middle of the pool stands a shallow sculpted saucer. On its rim nymphs have disposed themselves, drawing their knees protectively together, and Diana props her right foot while one of the nymphs dries her ankle with a cloth. The feet of Diana and the nymphs display that parting between the big toe and its next neighbour that marks people whose shoes are secured by a thong there.

The masonry, as old, presumably, as the story and its personages, though the immortal goddess is ageless, lapses. The squared column is out of true if the picture edge is true. The saucer-shaped bath lists to the left. Actaeon has not stepped on it but it behaves like a floating landing-stage in Venice which he is weighing down at the side of the picture he has entered.

The composition of the *Diana and Actaeon* is a brilliant tilt. In relation both to the water that crosses the picture diagonally at ground level and to the rectangle described by the picture's edges, the components tilt downwards and to the left, in keeping with the list of the saucer-shaped stonework. If the slung curtain that occurs in each Diana picture makes the scene of the gang's bath into a stage, Titian has chosen to dress not the actors but their architectural surroundings in period. The stonework is Romano-Greek, but unlike the people who inhabit it in the paintings it is not young. The architecture is now

160

so old, so rubbed, so uneven that it is on the point of sinking into the ground, a monument of what Sonnet 64 calls, with technological, metaphysically poetic exactitude about archaeology, an 'outworn, buried age'.

Titian's baroque masterpieces on the theme of Diana are, indeed, deeply Shakespearean. Shakespeare, too, was a plunderer of Ovid. More: I find it impossible not to believe that he knew Titian's Diana paintings either in engraving or by extremely detailed report.

Whereas Titian pairs his depictions of the two metamorphosis stories occasioned, directly and indirectly, by Diana, Shakespeare seems, in *Twelfth Night*, to conflate them. Orsino is by (Italian) name a Little Bear; and he declares that when his eyes did see Olivia first 'That instant was I turn'd into a hart:/And my desires like fell and cruel hounds/E'er since pursue me.'

The metamorphosis alike of Actaeon and of Callisto's Little-Bear son wreaks ironic vengeance, of a kind respecters of the rights of other-than-human animals often wish some magic would accomplish, on a huntsman who inflicts wanton deaths and torments.

The dumbness of Actaeon turned into a dumb animal is the myth's (as it might be a dream's) representation of impotence: the baroque death of desire in the orgasm that satisfies it.

Yet Diana herself is a hunter. In mythology she escapes vengeance. When, however, Shakespeare, invoking both magic and dream, invents a comic metamorphosis to set beside the dire ones collected by Ovid, she does not escape some comic indignity. Actaeon's metamorphosis begins, according to Ovid, with his head, and it is when he sees his reflexion in water that he recognises what is happening to him. Titian followed his *Diana and Actaeon* poetry with another in which only the head of Actaeon is yet a stag's. When Shakespeare transformed Bottom into an ass, he borrowed from Ovid (and perhaps from painters) the head-only metamorphosis that is practical in the theatre.

The person who is humiliated by her infatuation with Bottom in his ass's head is the moon goddess Diana, herself transformed.

She still wields magic. She is no longer virginal but she is capable, in her dispute with Oberon, of resuming a sort of virginity ('I have forsworn his bed and company') and of scattering the quivering disdain Diana points at Callisto. The consequences of her anger are those of the moon who 'Pale in her anger washes all the air'. The consequences of her contentment are 'moonlight revels'. Her athletic nymphs have changed into a mixed-sex school and shrunk to fairy courtiers, who defend her no longer from men but from spotted snakes, newts, blind-worms and hedgehogs. Yet her courtiers still hunt.

It is in his narration of the events that issued in the metamorphosis of Actaeon that Ovid names the moon goddess whom Shakespeare plucked and re-made. At the beginning of the passage where Actaeon blunders into the bathing scene, Ovid calls Diana by one of her rarest names, a reference to her Titan-born ancestry: Titania.

For Titian's Actaeon, the indeed proud Diana is indeed 'ill met' — but not, as Titania is for Oberon, by moonlight. Actaeon steps from sunny day under the worn-out architectural canopy that so inadequately shields the nymphs' bath, and its shadow falls on his flesh with the chill of the tomb.

Yet Titian has, by a beautiful and poetic conceit, created within his sunny scene a miniature night sky against which Diana appears. At her right, one of the nymphs dries her. At her left, nearer the front of the picture, her black attendant, in profile to the spectator, tends Diana and stares at the invading Actaeon.

Diana, a pearly full moon rather than the crescent emblem she wears on her head in both pictures, is set against the black skin, the night-sky skin, of her attendant ('Nigra sum sed formosa'). From the ear that the attendant turns, in profile, to the spectator an earring hangs. Her other ear is concealed; but the jewel in her right ear is Diana.

That conceit Shakespeare adopted in detail from Titian: for the indoor night scene where Romeo first sees Juliet, remarks that she doth teach the torches to burn bright and adds: 'It seems she hangs upon the cheek of night/Like a rich jewel in an Ethiop's ear.'

Titian's Diana hangs upon the cheek of her Ethiop attendant: a rich jewel indeed, of a kind much prized at the time of

Titian and Shakespeare. She bulges as women regularly do but regular pearls do not. She is a baroque pearl.

5

A National Anthem

Using the word *numbers* in the sense in which the infant Alexander Pope lisped in numbers, Dryden declared:

> 'The Numbers of Poetry and Vocal Musick are sometimes so contrary, that in many places I have been oblig'd to cramp my Verses, and make them rugged to the Reader, that they may be harmonious to the Hearer: Of which I have no Reason to repent me, because these sorts of Entertainment are principally design'd for the Ear and Eye; and therefore in Reason my Art, on this occasion, ought to be subservient to his.'

'His' was Henry Purcell's, the 'occasion' the collaboration in 1691 of Dryden and Purcell in the creation of *King Arthur: Or, The British Worthy, A Dramatick Opera*.

You could scarcely frame a more explicit declaration that Dryden considered his part in the matter secondary to Purcell's.

Yet when, in the 1970s, *King Arthur* was produced in a London opera house for the first time for two centuries, the programme chose to contradict Dryden directly and to tell a direct lie to the audience. Dryden, it said, 'never considered Purcell as an equal colleague but as someone who, along with the scenery and costumes, was a necessary adjunct to his drama'.

The baroque, if I am right, gives artistic form to ambivalent emotions. The manner in which one of its great occasions was revived, after perennial neglect, demonstrates the inartistic and often incoherent ambivalence that its revivalists of the 1970s provoked in its admirers.

There was an enormous accession of experience. If you lived in the South of England, you could actually see, at Colchester in 1978, a play by Aphra Behn, *The Rover*, in performance. In London theatres, halls and churches or cathedrals sensibly used as halls, you could acquaint yourself with the music of

163

Heinrich Schütz and G. P. Telemann, hear, in an aptly comely church, Saint John's, Smith Square, Opera da Camera's performance of Dryden's magnificent *Secular Masque* in the pleasing musical setting which William Boyce gave it some 47 years after Dryden's death, and become familiar with the full oeuvre of Mozart, thanks to the addition virtually to the repertory of his *opere serie*, and with the oeuvre of Monteverdi.

Those opportunities delighted the not massive yet not inconsiderable number of people, of whom I am one, for whom they were both desirable and indispensable. For every gross that exists of persons who can pick their way through musical notation, follow the full score of an opera while it is performed and enjoy the score of a work they know in the silence of their own reading head, you would be hard put to it to find one who can form from the score of a work he has never heard a firm enough impression of what it would be like in performance for him to judge whether or not he would enjoy hearing and seeing it performed.

As a matter of fact, although the skill required is less specialised and seems much lesser, something of the same is true of reading plays. Few great playwrights have followed Bernard Shaw's rational and patient act of publishing his plays in a form that makes them accessible to readers whose only accomplishment is that they can read.

Conductors, instrumentalists and singers made, by trying, great advances towards the rediscovery of an idiom in which to perform baroque music. It was the overseer powers in the baroque revival who often betrayed a curious mistrust of the artist they professed to be reviving. Clearly, they considered the artist whose talent had attracted them to be a great baby, who, capable of alluring an audience into the theatre, had not the smallest idea of how to hold it there. You can recognise a revivalist by his obsessional dread of leaving an audience alone with the music he revives, a procedure he believes would prompt an immediate and bored walkout. The audiences of the 1970s were therefore often given plushily and anachronistically orchestrated Monteverdi, orchestral preludes to Mozart's operatic arias interrupted by 'business' designed to divert the audience from the music it had chosen and paid to hear, realignments of the structural components of operatic drama — and simple lies.

The charm and greatness of *King Arthur* had to be glimpsed through the various realignments in the London performance and the programme's declaration that it 'could never have been called an opera'. That you would think a lie scarcely worth telling. It *was* called an opera: by Dryden and by whoever wrote the words 'K. Arthur an Opera' on the title-page of the earliest (1698–9) extant copy of the manuscript score.

Presumably the unspoken assumption was that anything that does not conform to the pattern of *Cav* and *Pag* cannot be an opera. The musical flow of *King Arthur* is interspersed with spoken dialogue. The same is true of *Die Zauberflöte* and *Die Entführung aus dem Serail*, which under that rule could never have been called operas either.

The programme spoke of 'John Dryden, a very much more eminent man in his day than Henry Purcell'. Plucking down the eminence then of either artist will not set up the eminence now of the other: and the facts do not accord with any such balancing act. Purcell was entitled to an official salary all his adult life. Yet he often had trouble in drawing it. At the accession of William and Mary he was required to provide the 'supplementary organ' at the coronation. Dryden was defrocked of his Poet Laureateship. He returned, with *King Arthur*, to writing for the theatre in an attempt to earn a living.

Purcell lived a comparatively short, Dryden a comparatively long time. Purcell's death at the age of 36 in 1695 was mourned by Dryden in a poem, *On the death of Mr. Purcell*, that calls him 'The godlike man'. He was buried in Westminster Abbey. So, in 1700, was Dryden, who lived to be 69. The funeral pomp was subscribed to by upper-class notables including the Lord Halifax to whom *King Arthur* was dedicated. Lord Halifax thus, Pope later pointed out, 'help'd to bury whom he help'd to starve'.

Dryden's dedicatory letter to the libretto of *King Arthur* records: 'There was nothing better, than what I intended, but the Musick: which has since arriv'd to a greater Perfection in *England*, than ever formerly; especially passing through the Artful Hands of Mr. *Purcel*, who has Compos'd it with so great a Genius, that he has nothing to fear but an ignorant, ill-judging Audience.'

By the 1970s Dryden's reputation had much to fear but nothing more than an audience misinformed by a programme written by someone who had not troubled to read Dryden's dedicatory letter, which is prefaced to the Purcell Society's edition of the score.

The restoration of Purcell to the repertory has been attempted for some time (the original supporters of the Purcell Society included Gustav Holst and Robert Bridges) and with considerable success in lodging some of his work in the repertory of Europe. Britain should not suppose, however, that it has discharged its responsibility to him as a great artist with the naming after him of a recital auditorium on the South Bank. Not that art is national. Baroque art, couched in the most international of styles, is unsusceptible to nationalism. *King Arthur* is national, in the manner of allusive and idiomatic comedy, but not nationalistic. For the good name of literary works or of the literary and dramatic components in operas a prime responsibility does, however, fall on the people in whose native language the work is written.

Both Purcell and Dryden now need a decent production of *King Arthur*, perhaps with the spoken dialogue cut, though sensitively, if its entirety would amount to too long an evening or if no one can master an idiom in which to present it. To restore this part of their heritage to the people who speak English we perhaps need a minister for the arts bold enough and benevolently despotic enough to withdraw public funds from British opera companies unless within a year one of them mounts an artistically respectable *King Arthur*. Dryden needs something further but less expensive. Public funds should be withdrawn from British theatre companies unless within six months they all promise to put *All for Love* reverently away in a drawer for the next twenty-five years and one of them puts on one of Dryden's other plays. I think *Aureng-Zebe* would be a good place to begin. *All for Love* is a good play but the present generation of theatrical powers will use it only to demonstrate to audiences that *Antony and Cleopatra* is a magnificent play. The message is true but better imparted by *Antony and Cleopatra*.

Britain owes two hundred years of unpaid tribute to Dryden, a great poet who is also the originator of the flexible, informal English discursive prose which literate discursive writers in English have, whether or not they know it, been using ever since.

Handel's triumphant dealings with Dryden's great poems were accomplished after Dryden's death. If you will blink for a moment, more or less reluctantly, over Gilbert and Sullivan, it is probable that *King Arthur* is the only masterpiece created in Britain by the live collaboration of two supreme artists.

It contains, moreover, a natural national anthem. Our present anthem is an historical curio of a not unendearing kind that allows virtuoso arrangers and conductors to starch and iron it spectacularly. Its obvious tune, however, would bore a kindergarten percussion band before it had finished the second repetition. Its naif doggerel, if, forcing yourself through repetitions, you penetrate to the later verses, turns out to be of a bellicosity that has embarrassed many Britons.

It will signal that Britain has recovered its aspiration to a civilised state when the present national anthem is relegated to being used only during years that bear even numbers and in the odd-numbered years the *King Arthur* alternative is used instead. Purcell has provided it with one of those simple, exactly right tunes that seem the utterance of a music-making angel. Dryden's verses are boastful, which national anthems are obliged to be, and elegant and amusing into the bargain.

> Fairest Isle, all Isles Excelling,
>   Seat of Pleasures, and of Loves;
> *Venus*, here, will chuse her Dwelling,
>   And forsake her *Cyprian* Groves.
>
> Every Swain shall pay his Duty,
>   Grateful every Nymph shall prove;
> And as these Excel in Beauty,
>   Those shall be Renown'd for Love.

Second Figure, Fourth Mood

'Baroque', according to the *Shorter Oxford English Dictionary*, entered the English language in 1818 and corresponds to the Portuguese 'barroco', a word of unknown origin applied to rough or irregularly-shaped pearls (of the kind called baroque).

I have no idea why the *r*, which is single in other languages, is doubled in Portuguese. All the same, I think I know the origin of the word. It is an invented word, one of a series of code-names in which the vowels and the order in which they occur, many of the consonants between them, the consonant, if there is one, on which a code-name ends and the initial letters all have significance in a fairly complex code.

The code and the code-names belong to the lore of the schoolmen. ('To schoolmen I bequeath my doubtfulness', says Donne's metaphysical poem *The Will*.) The schoolmen's endeavour was to render Aristotle's teaching about logic assimilable and workable.

Aristotle groups syllogisms in four figures according to the four possible structural patterns. In each figure, a number of sub-patterns is possible, each called a mood of the syllogism in that figure. For each of the nineteen valid (correctly reasoned, in accordance with the rules of the syllogism) moods the schoolmen devised a code-name.

The code-name of the first mood of the first figure is Barbara. The three vowels in the name indicate that the three propositions (statements in logical form, where a Subject Term is linked to a Predicate Term by a copula that is part of the verb *to be*) that comprise a syllogism are all A propositions, following the structural model 'All X is Z'. The code-name of the fourth mood of the first figure is Ferio. A syllogism in that mood consists, in descending order as you set them out, of an E, an I and an O proposition, taking respectively the skeleton forms 'No X is Z', 'Some X is Z' and 'Some X is not Z'.

Of the four figures of the syllogism Aristotle considers only the first to be perfect, in the sense that its correctitude and the sufficiency of its reasoning are self-declaratory. However, it is possible to 'reduce' a syllogism in any of the valid moods of the three imperfect figures to a first-figure syllogism yielding the same conclusion. What you have proved by valid but imperfect means is thus proved by an argument in perfect form.

The process of reducing syllogisms is logicians' equivalent of doing sums. From any proposition correctly marshalled in logical form certain 'immediate inferences' can be made. If you are given an A proposition that reads 'All humans are bipeds', you also know, though you will scarcely think it worth remarking on unless you are doing a logical exercise, the I proposition 'Some humans are bipeds'. The inference is 'immediate' in the sense that in order to establish it you do not need to adduce extra facts or to go through an argumentative procedure.

In using Aristotelian logic as though it were a calculator or computer, the schoolmen were using a machine that had no material embodiment and no memory except the human one of the operator. The code-names of the moods of the syllogism were devised to help that memory. The initial letter of the code-name for a mood in one of the imperfect figures tells you to which mood in the perfect first figure you can reduce your imperfect-figure syllogism. The internal and, when they exist, which is not always, the consonants at the ends of the code-names tell you which type of 'immediate inference' to draw and in what order to place the resultant propositions in the new, first-figure syllogism you are constructing.

By obeying the instructions encapsulated in the code-name of the syllogism he has to reduce, the operator of the logic-machine can, by 'direct' reduction, convert all but two of the fifteen moods in the imperfect figures into corresponding syllogisms in the appropriate moods of the first and perfect figure.

Recently (in comparison, at least, with the long history of logic), logicians have devised methods of directly reducing even the two recalcitrant moods and have equipped those moods with new code-names encapsulating newly coined code-instructions. In traditional logic, however, the recalcitrant moods, one of which is in the second figure and the other in the third, can be reduced only indirectly.

You begin the indirect reduction by pretending to assume (assuming for the sake of argument) the truth of a proposition that contradicts the conclusion of the original syllogism. You combine your contradictory proposition with one of the premisses of the original syllogism. You thus construct a new syllogism, in the first figure, whose conclusion contradicts the other premiss of the original syllogism in such a way as to demonstrate the truth of the original syllogism's conclusion.

To make them more easily memorable by the schoolmen, the code-names of the moods were embedded in five Latin hexameters, which scan exactly like, and obey the same rules of scansion as, the classical Latin hexamaters of Lucretius and Virgil.

Apart from occasionally describing them as medieval, logic textbooks of the 19th and 20th centuries seldom ascribe much in the way of dates or individuality to the schoolmen. However, one slim handbook, first published in 1937, W. A. Sinclair's *The Traditional Formal Logic*, says that the mnemonic hexameters were devised by William Shyreswood, chancellor of the diocese of Lincoln in the 'earlier half' of the 13th century, and that they 'passed into the logical tradition' as a result of being cited in the *Summulae Logicales* by his 'later contemporary, Petrus Hispanus, who became the Pope known variously as John XX or XXI'.

The same handbook states that, for nearly five hundred years after Shyreswood's death, the code-name of one of the two moods that had to be indirectly reduced was at Oxford given to the gatehouse and prison where vice-chancellors imprisoned 'disorderly' members of the university.

The mnemonic lines are in classical Latin, but the bulk of them consists of the code-names for the moods. Those, unlike proper names in Latin, cannot inflect. To alter their form would disturb the information coded in their letters. When the lines say in Latin that the third figure contains ('tertia . . . habet') this, that and the other moods, the code-names cannot make any attempt to go into the accusative case.

All the same, the code-names are Latinate or Latinish. Most of them are at least not impossible as pseudo-Latin. Indeed, though they cannot and are not meant to make sense in the context, at least two of the code-names are Latin words: Festino

170

(which is the first person singular of the present indicative of 'festinare', to hasten, and also the dative and the ablative masculine singular of the adjective 'festinus', hasty); and Barbara (forms of the feminine singular and of the neuter plural of the adjective 'barbarus', strange, barbarian, unintelligible in speech).

The scansion of the lines reveals where the stress falls in the code-names. The first mood of the second figure, Cesare, is a dactyl, stressed on the first syllable, just as the word is when it is an Italian name descended from the Latin Caesar; but whether the stressed Ce- has the Italian initial sound *ch* or a French *s* sound scansion cannot disclose.

Although they stick to the classical Latin habit of not rhyming, the lines seem to belong to the moment, which lasted for several centuries, when Latin deliquesced and was rechrystalised into several incipiently modern languages, a moment when Latin as a spoken language was maintaining a probably already slightly artificial existence because it was a vital vehicle for communication between speakers of the diverse modern languages that took its place.

There are variant versions but the gist of the mnemonic hexameters is, with the code-names of the moods accorded an initial capital:

> Barbara, Celarent, Darii, Ferioque prioris;
> Cesare, Camestres, Festino, Baroco secundae;
> tertia Darapti, Disamis, Datisi, Felapton,
> Bocardo, Ferison habet; quarta insuper addit
> Bramantip, Camenes, Dimaris, Fesapo, Fresison.

Only two of the code-names contain an internal *c*. The coded significance of the internal *c* is that the mood could not be directly reduced but had to undergo the slow-chapt process of indirect reduction. The two moods thus coded are Baroco and Bocardo.

I conjecture that some perceptive and imaginative person, perhaps indeed Portuguese, perhaps a jeweller who had learnt logic, noticed the resemblance between the two sore-thumb moods of the syllogism and, in the first place, the sort of pearl that owes its attractiveness and value to its not conforming with the classically regular shape of pearls and, eventually, works of art in a style that creates beauty by not conforming to the classically accepted modes.

Either of the two code-names for those two syllogistic moods would have served the metaphorical purpose. I expect Baroco was chosen because it comes earlier in the mnemonic lines and in the order of the figures of the syllogism. Perhaps it is a good thing that accident has left a vacant slot, now that it is no longer occupied by an Oxford prison. May the resourceful human species contrive to stay extant long enough and stay civilised enough to explore and disclose the at present inconceivable nature of works of art couched in the bocardo idiom, which, to unimaginative and conformist minds alive at that time, will no doubt seem to be couched in barbara.